THE CRAZY DERVISH AND THE POMEGRANATE TREE

Books by Farnoosh Moshiri

The Crazy Dervish and the Pomegranate Tree
The Bathhouse
At the Wall of the Almighty

THE CRAZY DERVISH AND THE POMEGRANATE TREE

Farnoosh Moshiri

Black Heron Press
Post Office Box 95676
Seattle, Washington 98145
www.blackheronpress.com

"The Wall" was originally published in *Gulf Coast*. "The Dark End of the Orchard" was anthologized in *Red Boots and Attitude: Poems and Stories by Texas Women Writers*. "The Pool" was published in *Asheghane* and anthologized in *Red Boots and Attitude*. "The Bricklayer" was anthologized in *A World Between: Poems, Short Stories, and Essays by Iranian-Americans*.

Copyright 2004 Farnoosh Moshiri. All rights reserved. No part of this book may be reproduced in any form or by any electronic or mechanical means, including information storage and retrieval systems, without permission in writing from the publisher, except by a reviewer who may quote brief passages in a review.

The characters in this book are fictitious. Any similarities to real persons, living or dead, are coincidental and not intended by the author.

ISBN 0-930773-70-5

Black Heron Press
Post Office Box 95676
Seattle, Washington 98145
www.blackheronpress.com

For Anoosh and Esfand

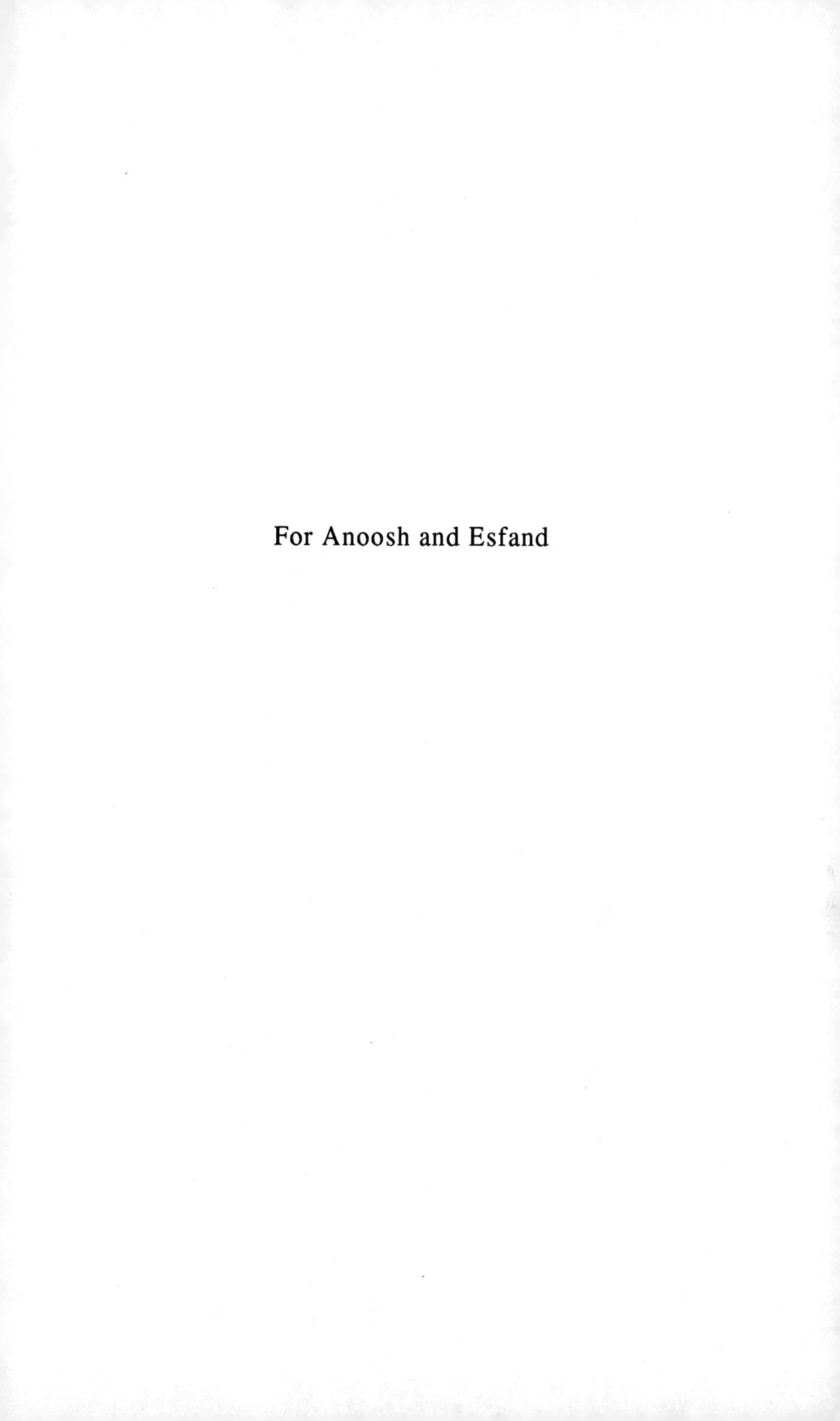

ACKNOWLEDGEMENTS

In 1987, after four years of exile in Afghanistan and India, I sought asylum in the United States. I'd been a published playwright and fiction writer in Iran, but now I had to begin again. This was not an easy task, but I was determined to succeed.

With the exception of "On The Rooftop," which was written in the spring of 2001, the stories in this collection were written in the early and mid-nineties, when I had just switched the language of my writing from Farsi (Persian) to English. During this period, I was a graduate student in the University of Houston's creative writing program. With the publication of this book, I'd like to thank those friends and teachers who encouraged me to write in English. I was a nonnative speaker who needed to raise her voice and tell stories that perhaps no one had told.

They are enemies of hope, my love,
Of flowing water
And the fertile tree
Of life growing and unfolding.
Death has branded them
Rotting teeth, decaying flesh—
And soon they will be dead and gone for good.

—Nazim Hikmet

CONTENTS

The Wall, 13

The Bricklayer, 26

Crossing, 54

The Pillar, 60

Ali The Little, 64

On the Rooftop, 78

The Pool, 96

The Dark End of the Orchard, 101

The Story of Our Life, 115

The Unbelievable Story of My Grandfather's Wife, 124

The Danger of Galapagos, 139

The Crazy Dervish and the Pomegranate Tree, 149

THE WALL

We sat in two rows facing each other in a black van. We were twelve men, six on each side. The bearded guard covered our eyes with large scarves. Like a magician he pulled a scarf out of his pocket, wrapped it around someone's eyes, tied it tight at the back, pulled the next one out, and then the next. I was the last person, the twelfth one. The guard, who was already tired of this tedious job, covered my eyes carelessly. I could see everything; the scarf was slipping down on my nose.

There was no window in the back, but I could see the driver's window; he had rolled it down. It was September and the breeze was fragrant. Damascus roses bloom in this month, I thought. Around this time of the year the schools open. I remembered how I always walked to school early in the morning and felt the same fragrant breeze on my face. Even then I was conscious of the Damascus roses.

I was happy that my blindfold was loose and I could see everything.

The van bumped up and down. It was a country road, no asphalt. I saw the olive trees passing by. It was not dawn yet. Everything was gray, not quite dark and not quite bright.

Some of us were dozing off. Tilted heads wobbled on thin necks. One of us hummed a forbidden song, a love song about a revolutionary who asks his lover to kiss him good-bye, because he is going to be executed:

"Kiss me, kiss me for the last time... May God protect you! I'm going to my fate..."

We couldn't talk; I'm sure we would have, if there had been a wall between the guards and us, but there wasn't. We couldn't look at each other either and talk with our eyes; our eyes were covered. Mine were not; my scarf was loose and was now on my nose.

It wasn't that we had no idea where they were taking us. If we could have talked, we would have shared our guesses. The strongest possibility was that they were transferring us to a different prison, the one that was outside the city, the worst, the one with modern torture equipment. The second possibility was that they were taking us somewhere to work, to build a new prison, maybe. The third was that they were taking us somewhere in the desert where they would hand us machine guns and force us to shoot the other political prisoners—those who had been sentenced to death.

I was sure that the others were considering

the same scenarios behind their black blindfolds or in the dark abyss of their dreams. There was no other possibility. Why would they drag us out of our cell before dawn, cover our eyes and take us to who knew where? None of us had been tried yet; all of us were in a temporary situation—the stage after the tortures and before the trial. My intestines, which were bleeding as the result of a certain method of anal torture, had only recently begun to heal. They couldn't possibly execute us; that was out of the question.

The olive trees were passing. When I was little, every summer we went to this resort area by the sea. My father had an old VW bug. My sister and I sat in the little hollow space under the rear window. We sat face-to-the-window and watched the road. All the way I looked at the olive trees passing at the sides of the road. They were white, light green, gray, green-gray and white again, strange colors for trees. My father hummed the old forbidden song all the way: "Kiss me, kiss me, for the last time... May God protect you! I'm going to my fate...." My mother peeled the tender skin of a slim, green cucumber, cut it vertically into four long pieces, poured salt on them and gave each of us a piece to eat. She peeled another cucumber and then another, till our little car smelled fresh with the grassy scent of young, tender cucumbers. Sometimes my father had a bad headache and Mother laid the cool, green skins of cucumber on his forehead. He looked like an Indian chief in the western movies and we laughed at him. Cucumber skins absorb the pain, my mother believed. When Father felt better, he hummed his old love song that he remembered from when he was a rebel.

I loved the part where he raised his voice dramatically, became sentimental, and told his lover that he was lost in the middle of an unknown sea:

"In the midst of the storm, I'm wandering with the boatmen.... We have sacrificed our lives, that's why we can't keep our promises...."

The van bumped up and down. The sky was still dark; dawn was not to come. One of us was snoring and that made me remember my dream. Last night I dreamed the strangest dream of all in my three years in prison. I dreamed about a woman I knew once, one of our friends, a woman whose whereabouts I do not know and probably will never know. She was my friend's wife. She fell in love with someone else and she and my friend got divorced. But her lover left her after a few months. She was lonely and was living in a dark apartment facing a wall. When she looked out her window, there was this wall right in front of her; a bricklayer was busy working on it all the time, twenty-four hours a day, nonstop, laying bricks on top of bricks. The wall grew taller and taller everyday. It got to a level where she couldn't see the sky anymore.

After her lover left, I used to go and visit her. She was quiet most of the time, depressed maybe, because of what had happened to her, and the wall. I did all the talking. I wanted to keep her current. Those were the crucial days: a revolution, a war, and several coups and assassinations, one after another. I considered it my revolutionary duty to visit her and not let her become politically passive. Was I attracted to her? In a strange way, not quite sexual—maybe. She was a mystery to me, completely closed, living in a world unknown and inaccessible. I wanted to open her up, unfold her, but I didn't know how. I became so obsessed with my own verbal ability that instead of getting her to talk I did all the talking myself. I began the conversation, then talked so much that my own words drowned me in a whirlpool of never-ending monologue. Most of the time I found myself spinning in this whirlpool, talking forever, while she sat there motionless, listening to me, not even blinking. This passivity encouraged me even more and I plunged deeper into myself, believing that I was impressing her by my eloquence.

    Night after night I visited her and talked. I didn't learn anything about her. She remained closed up in her many folds to the end. One evening I stayed late. I finished talking about politics and started a new subject: men and women. Then I led the subject to sex and gradually to more private matters. I even asked her some personal questions, like whether she'd ever had good sex with her husband or the man she loved, which she didn't answer. Then I talked about my own sexual life, my ex-wife, our unhappy marriage, and so on. At two in the morning I asked her if she wanted to sleep with me. She said no. I insisted; she seemed quite detached and cold, absent in a way. But, for some reason (maybe extreme depression) she was completely passive. She could have asked me to leave, which I'd have done immediately, but she didn't. So I kept insisting.

    By three in the morning she was very tired. I'll never forget her eyes. They were red, like someone who has cried for hours. She sat on her bed, leaning back against the wall, at times even dozing off. I talked constantly, but she was withdrawn, having gone somewhere far away from me. In the short intervals when I stopped talking, we heard the bricklayer laying bricks on top of bricks. He used his trowel to spread the mortar,

flatten it, and lay another brick. It was dark. We couldn't see the wall, but we could feel it.
At four, I persuaded her to sleep with me. She was exhausted. I had exhausted her. She gave up resisting only because she was tired and wanted to get rid of me and get some sleep. She said, "Okay." No, she put it this way; she said, "You can have me, come; then go and leave me alone."
I don't know what had gotten into me that night. I wasn't in love with her. I didn't want sex either. I just wanted to break the ice, go inside her, unfold her, understand her maybe. I made love to her; no, not that. Whatever it was, it was unpleasant. She was frozen under me, mummified. The moment I entered her, I froze too. When I buttoned up my pants, I felt awkward, ugly. The last thing she told me before I left, the last thing she told me ever, was, "Turn the lights out!"
It was dawn when I left her apartment. The wall was so high I couldn't see the top. The bricklayer was up there in the sky. Walking in the gray alley, I pictured her lying in bed, the palm of her right hand under her cheek, facing the wall, witnessing how it was growing tall, blocking the bright morning sun, reflecting only a dim grayish light.
I saw her later, several times, in the meetings and mass demonstrations. She acted like

nothing had ever happened between us. She never came close to me, but didn't hide herself either. I was there, one among many, a friend, not a close one though; an acquaintance to whom you never talk, but you may work with or share ideas. Several times I was going to tell her that I needed to talk to her, but I never did. What did I want to tell her? Did I want to apologize? Did I want to make sure that I hadn't hurt her feelings? Or maybe I just wanted to ask the question: "What happened to that wall? Is he still laying the bricks?"

But I never talked to her again, and it happened that the bearded guards attacked all of our organizations and houses. Most of us were arrested, some escaped from the country, and a few committed suicide.

I don't know her whereabouts. Was she arrested or did she manage to escape? She couldn't possibly have stayed in that apartment; although the wall was tall, the guards could still find her.

So last night I dreamed this strange dream. There we were, both of us, standing in front of her window, looking at the wall. The bricklayer was up there laying bricks.

I said, "I've come here to—"

She said, "Sh... sh... don't talk, just listen."

I listened. It was the sound of the bricklayer's trowel flattening the mortar, and then dumping a brick on the mud. It was a constant, monotonous sound.
I said, "How tall is it going to get?"
She said, "Who knows?"
I said, "How do you feel now?"
She said, "Calm, I'm calm."
Now the bricklayer fell down. It took him quite a while to get to the ground. His scalp opened wide like a ripe, red watermelon and his brain slipped smoothly out. I screamed, clawed my face and cried; I yelled and howled like a baby. Like an orphan, like somebody lost, I shed tears. It was as though I had no hope in this world whatever. She looked at me, calm; she didn't even blink. Now she looked at the wall again. I thought to myself, She has never forgiven me. She will never forgive me and can never be kind to me. At that moment in my dream, the only thing which could have saved me from that intolerable misery, that feeling of total ruin, would have been her tender affection. But she didn't give it to me. I stood there crying like a baby and she watched the wall as though nothing had happened.
When I woke up, two bearded guards were standing at the iron gate of the cell. The small eye-window on the ceiling was black. The night was

still deep. The guards told us to leave our things in the cell and come out. It was a long way to dawn when we got in the van.

The olive trees were white, light green, gray, green-gray and white, tender twigs bending with the gentle breeze. One of us snored. I knew who he was. He was always sleeping. In the past three years he had gradually reached a stage where nothing was important to him. Transferring to a worse jail? So be it. Building a prison with our own hands? So be it. Being executed? So be it. He was not himself anymore. Long ago in the torture chambers, when they took his soul out of him, they took all the pain out at the same time. He no longer felt the pain, so they stopped bothering him. Now, not knowing where we were going and not caring either, in the dark vacuum of his meaningless dreams he was snoring.

  The van bumped up and down. Now I could see the desert; it was the end of the road; the van stopped. So this is the case, I thought, we are going to kill our own friends. My heart climbed into my throat and reached my mouth. Am I able to do this? How? How can I fire at my own comrades? At anyone? Friend or no friend? Am I able to fire at all? What about the others? Can they do this? What if we resist? They will kill us on the spot. Who cares, huh? Do the authorities care? The bearded guards can tell them that we rioted and they had to kill us. Meanwhile the guards came into the van and removed our blindfolds. We looked around, at the desert, at each other. One of us suddenly shouted, "Comrades, they are going to execute us!"

A guard hit him on the mouth with the back of his hand. His big gold ring with the picture of the Great Leader carved on it tore our friend's lips; blood gushed out. Then they pushed us out of the van. The same man with his mouth full of blood shouted again, "They are going to kill us before our trial, comrades! This is against the law!"

This is impossible, I thought—out of the question. I looked around; there was no other van, no other prisoners, no one but us, the guards, and the endless desert all around, bluish-gray, breathing silently in the last minutes of the night.

They prodded and hit us with the butts of their guns. Where are they taking us? I thought. What's the difference? Why don't they kill us right here? Then I felt my knees buckling under me and I collapsed. I'd never have collapsed if I hadn't seen the wall. There it was, in the middle of the desert, the tall brick wall, reaching the sky. It wasn't just a wall, any wall, it was the wall of my nightmares, the wall behind the woman's window, the wall the bricklayer was building, the wall that he fell off, the wall that made me cry in the last dream of my life.

They dragged us to the wall and made us stand there facing it; they stepped back. We stood face to the wall, our noses almost touching it. I smelled the fresh mortar and heard the monotonous sound of the trowel smoothing the mud. The sound came from the very top of the wall, from the sky, saying something like "swoosh ... swoosh ... swoosh...." It was as if we stood there forever.

I felt the fragrant breeze of September. I heard my father humming, "In the midst of the storm... wandering with the boatmen..." I saw the green-gray leaves of the olive trees waving with the breeze. I felt the cool soothing touch of the cucumber skins on my forehead. I touched the tall, dark, shadowy body of the woman I hurt, the only woman I ever hurt in my life. Then I heard the clicks. One of us whispered, "O God, have mercy on us!" Someone else muttered, "Mother!" The comrade with the bloody mouth shouted, "Long live the Revolution!" And they fired.

We sat in two rows again, on the way back, six men on each side. They covered our eyes with the same black scarves. I was the first one. The bearded guard tied the scarf so tight that it hurt my head. I couldn't see anything. There was complete blackness. But I knew that some of us had fainted at the wall and had been dragged into the van. A couple of us were wet with pee and vomit. Nobody hummed anymore. Nobody dozed off—not even the man who slept all the time. I couldn't see the olive trees; I didn't want to see them, even if I could; I didn't want to see anything. The only thing I wanted was the cell; I wanted to go back to the cell and stay there forever. I thought, It's good that we are going back to our cell. I felt a warmth and security I hadn't felt for years. I thought, After a while we will recover from this false execution and I'll ask my friends if they also noticed the wall in the desert, if the wall was really there.

The van bumped up and down, taking us to our cell. I heard the sun slowly coming out from behind the remote edge of the desert, lighting the world. I felt its fragrant honey taste in my mouth, the taste of life. But I could not see the dawn; the black scarf separated me from the sun.

THE BRICKLAYER
For Nani

It all looked like the fragments of a shattered dream—the dusk, the dark indigo sky, and the way the airport mini-bus drove them over an endless road with the speed of light. He craned his neck, but couldn't see the driver. It was as if the bus drove itself. He clawed the front seat and ignored his daughters who sat on either side of him, looking at him lovingly, studying his aged face. The twins hadn't seen him for many years.

Could this all be true? It was more like one of his recurring nightmares: a remote land with long roads, fast-moving cars, tall buildings, dark corridors, and elevators which always stuck between floors. Now the bus drove through a crooked street, making several rights and lefts before it finally stopped.

The girls helped him out, held his arms, and walked him through a sand-covered courtyard to a basement. Everywhere it was dark. He couldn't see, but could hear chains clinking. He wanted to remove the eye patch from his bad eye, but his daughters held his arms tightly. He couldn't speak. In this dark basement there was an elevator. They took him inside. The elevator didn't have a door. Someone pushed a button and the metal box first squeaked, then groaned, and took them up to the house. He wasn't even sure whose house this strange place was. Did it belong to Abi, the daughter who was a teacher and had a husband, or Bibi, the other one, who didn't have a job and was divorced? But it didn't matter. All he needed was to be alone, to remove his eye patch, to let the light in. He had to let the light inside his head.

So this was America. And this place was where he had to stay "for a little while," as they were saying, until his son-in-law would find him and his wife a house. "A house," he murmured; then he said, "Home," and repeated this word so many times until it lost its meaning.

"Home, home, home, home," he murmured, and limped from one room to another, peering through all of the six windows of his daughter's house. He stood at the bedroom window, looking at the neighbor's yard. The black man's roof was cracked, sinking, almost falling on his head. In the middle of the yard, he had a big bathtub, yellow enamel chipped. He had gathered some rain water. Why? the old man wondered, but again he didn't want to think hard to find the answer. He stood in front of the kitchen window and looked at his daughter's yard, a big sand-covered space with only one small flowerbed on the left. The fresh dark soil showed that the bed had been recently and hastily prepared. Now the dog was digging the pansies out. He peered from another window and saw a bar with blinking red neon. Some men in tatters went in and out. Where was this house? He wondered. Was his daughter poor? He looked around to see if anyone was there, if he could remove the eye patch. But his wife sat close to him, unpacking the suitcases. She took their son's framed picture out, laid it in front of her on the table, and then started to fold or unfold clothes.

Mr. Parvin sat at the kitchen table to eat. His daughters, Abi and Bibi, kissed his cheeks. In a flash of memory he remembered them as little girls, twins, sitting on his lap, one on his right leg, the other on his left. He remembered the scent of their hair too, sweet and grassy at the same time. But he didn't want to remember more. All he wanted was to be left alone, but they wouldn't leave. What if they wouldn't give him a chance to be by himself? What if they'd stick to him all the time? Now they were talking about finding a place, a house. His son-in-law was going to show them a house with a yard so that Mr. Parvin could sit on a bench and watch the plants. "House," he said, smiled, and bent his head low on the plate, almost touching the food with the tip of his nose.

He ate as fast as he could, making munching and gulping sounds. He felt everyone's gaze on himself. His wife's burning eyes pierced his head. He raised his eyes. She motioned to him to lift his head and eat properly. He smiled and this time lifted the spoon so slowly that midway the soup spilled out. One of his daughters burst into tears, mumbling between sobs, loudly, hysterically, the way she used to cry and mumble when she was little, upsetting everybody. This was Bibi.

"What's... happened... to Baba?" She asked between hiccups.

Living in his daughter's house "for a little while" seemed like an eternity. So where was this house his son-in-law was going to show them? When his wife scrubbed his back in the bathtub he whispered, "The house..," and she whispered back, "Soon, soon." He didn't say anything, just touched his black eye patch with his wet fingers, as if wanting to remove it. His wife told him not to touch it. Then he sat motionless and let his wife remove the patch and shampoo his hair. All this massive white hair, this mass of useless hair. He vaguely remembered himself with his thick black hair, combed back and set with Vaseline. But he didn't want to remember more. He listened to the hollow sounds of the bathroom. His wife's heavy breathing, gasping almost, toiling to wash the heavy bulk of his body and his thick white mane. Through the curtain of water covering his face he glanced at the bathroom window with his good eye. His bad eye was shut tight. He was tempted to open it and let the light in, let the colors happen, let the bricklayer come. But he didn't; he kept the bad eye closed and his wife covered it with the patch again.

Since that first day he avoided the doorless elevator. His son-in-law insisted that he should use it to go down to the yard—it was safe. He was an engineer, designed and built the elevator just for Mr. Parvin's convenience, so that he wouldn't have to use the narrow steps. But the old man avoided the squeaky elevator. What if it would stop between the first floor and the basement, in the middle of the dark nowhere? He used the narrow stairway, took one step after another. Holding to the cold wall, he placed his good foot first, dragged his bad foot behind, and secured it next to the good one. It took him forever to get to the yard. He thought he'd lost most of his morning and felt angry. Mornings were when everybody finally went to work and his wife became busy with cooking and left him alone for a little while.

At last he was in the yard; he could enjoy himself. First he made sure that Gorgi, the huge gray dog, was chained. Then he limped up and down the yard several times, listening to the crackling of the sand under his shoes. He glanced at Gorgi several times to make sure he was asleep, or at least lying down peacefully, resting his head on his paws, watching him with sad eyes. He counted his trips to the gate and back to the steps—ten times. Then he sat on the steps and looked at the flower bed. In the empty place where the pansies were that Gorgi had dug out and chewed up they had planted some more. He had always loved pansies; he used to have them in his houses back home; maybe that was why his daughter had planted them. But now he didn't want to think about the pansies or his daughter. He just looked at the blossoms without feeling anything. They were carefully chosen. The colors were dark and light shades of blue-purple, the lavender of dusk. The large but fragile blossoms bent under their own weight, as if a row of shy girls stood in front of him, posing self-consciously. But enough of them, he thought. His precious morning was passing. His wife would call him any minute to go up and have lunch.

He was alone, the sun was in the sky, the dog was asleep. Now he could remove the eye patch, allowing his guest to appear. But first the lights would come. Back home the doctor had explained that the reason he saw these lights and images was because of his torn retina. The light hit this crack, creating many colorful shapes like a kaleidoscope. He had a kaleidoscope in his eye and he could entertain himself any time he wanted. Just by sitting in the sun and removing the eye patch he could have the whole world before him. When his wife first saw him doing this she scolded him for damaging his eye even more. But then she left him alone. She didn't know about the rest, though. No one knew that someone visited Mr. Parvin.

The bricklayer was simply called the bricklayer. He had no other name. He came into Mr. Parvin's life after he possessed the kaleidoscope, after he stopped speaking much. The bricklayer was a man in his forties with a sun-baked face, creased forehead, dark, piercing eyes and wide brown hands, clay and mortar dried on them. He was broad-shouldered. A worker.

"Good morning, my friend!"

"Good morning Mr. Parvin!" the bricklayer said.

"Sit here, on these steps."

"Thank you, Mr. Parvin."

"What's going on at home?"

"The same, sir. They're arresting more and more, locking people up."

"Even the old people?"
"Even the old ones like yourself."
"They arrested me once."
"I know, don't I?"

Mr. Parvin sighed, sat with the bricklayer and said nothing. His visits with the worker were like this. Relaxed and informal. Neither of them forced the other one to talk. They talked if there was a need to. Now he wasn't thinking about the prison or the prisoners. He didn't want to. Gazing at the pansies, relaxing, he just felt good and safe. His friend was next to him.

Evening at the dinner table, where his family sat around him, all talking at the same time, Mr. Parvin suddenly hit his knife hard on the china plate to make them be quiet. For a second, the shrieking voices of his daughters echoed in the silent kitchen. When finally everybody was quiet he stood up. Behind him, the kitchen window framed the orange glow of the fall sunset. Everybody stared at him, standing at the head of the table against the dusk. He could hear his wife's heart pulsing and see the blue vein on her temple throbbing with anxiety. What was he going to talk about? He hadn't said a full sentence since they'd arrived. Only a few scattered words now and then. His daughters thought that their father had lost his speech after the stroke.

"Grandpa wants to talk!" The little red-haired granddaughter broke the silence. This was Abi's daughter, the four-year-old freckle-face Mr. Parvin had tried to avoid since they'd arrived. Someone hushed her. He listened to the silence again. The dog down below rolled on the sand, his chain rattling. This constant sound of the chain made Mr. Parvin remember why he hit his knife on the plate. He had to tell them the truth. He had to tell his daughters everything.

"They took me there," he said. "Back home. They hit the heavy book on my head. The man said, 'Are you trying to become a hero, old man?' I said, 'No, sir!' Then they hit the book again. Here, let me show you!"

He rubbed the right side of his head. His daughters rushed to him. They took turns touching the spot, like when they were little and took turns sitting on his lap playing with his hair. Under their fingers, the bump felt like a hard walnut.

"They didn't hit him," his wife said calmly. "He always had that bump. When he was a kid, he fell out of a tree or off a wall or something," she said.

"They took me to the dark room," Mr. Parvin, still standing against the window, said, "They asked me where my son was. I said, 'My son is here, with you!'"

"What is all this about, Maman?" Bibi burst out.

"Why haven't you told us all this?" Abi echoed.

"After your brother escaped, they arrested your father," Mrs. Parvin said. "It was just a brief interrogation. They wanted to know where your brother was. That's all."

"They beat him!" Bibi said, sobbing loudly.

"With a heavy book! Here!" Mr. Parvin added.

"He is making this part up. They didn't hit him," Mrs. Parvin insisted.

"But his retina tore—" Abi said, and wiped her eyes.

"That was six months later," Mrs. Parvin explained. "Your brother was hiding for six months. Finally, they found him and locked him up. Your father had the stroke after he heard the news. The stroke did this to him, damaged the right side of his body and his right eye..." Now Mrs. Parvin wept into her napkin. "What a nightmare I went through. My son under torture, my husband paralyzed, none of you were there to help me."

"With a heavy book!" Mr. Parvin repeated. "And the man said, 'Are you trying to become a hero, old man?'"

The twins took their parents to the bedroom, gave them each a tranquilizer, and sat in the living room with the TV on, but mute. It was raining outside. They could hear the water pouring into the neighbor's bathtub. Sometimes a drunk sailor sang, coming out of the bar, sometimes Gorgi, now wet and impatient, shook himself, clattering his chain. The sisters sat for the long hours of the night, even after the red-haired girl and her father went to bed. They lit a candle in front of their brother's picture, remembering him in silence.

Now Mr. Parvin didn't mind if Gorgi sat at his foot, rubbing his wet muzzle against his pants. He said a few words to him and then removed the eye patch. When he looked around the yard with his eyes open he felt anxious. What if it wouldn't happen this time? Now he talked about this with Gorgi.

"Gorgi Khan, I'm going to cover my good eye and uncover my bad eye. Do you know what it means? It means that the lights and colors will come in. Aha... I'm covering the damn bastard. Oh, Gorgi, poor dog, I'm sorry for you. All you can see with your doggy eyes is black and white, isn't that so? Do you know what I'm seeing?

Hundreds of diamonds, circles, triangles, and nameless shapes in hundreds of colors. It's unbelievable! He is coming now. He is pushing the shapes aside and getting closer to me. You have to leave me, Mr. Gorgi. Go, my friend, make some space for my guest!" He pushed the dog and when the dog didn't move, he nudged him gently with the tip of his shoe. Now the bricklayer sat where the dog was sitting before and Mr. Parvin felt excited, overjoyed.

"You're here again, my friend. Welcome!"

"I'm here all right, Mr. Parvin. I'm here whenever you really want to see me."

"That's good. Very good. I'm not alone. You are my companion. My comrade. Now tell me about home. What's new?"

"Nothing is new, sir. The same things. Yesterday they stoned a man and a woman in a market place. They buried them up to their waists so that they wouldn't be able to run away. They stoned them to death."

"What's happening in prison?"

"Executions. Every day."

"Early mornings, huh?"

"Any time now. At sunset, too."

"How are they? The boys and the girls?"

"They are heroic, Mr. Parvin. They sing till the last minute."

"Did he sing, too?"
"He sang."
"You're saying this to make me happy, huh?"
"No. I was there, sir. He sang."

That evening at the table Mr. Parvin hit his knife on the plate again, making another brief speech. He told his daughters how the authorities executed their brother. He described the whole scene as if he had been there and witnessed it.

"Around five o'clock, they blindfolded them and took them out of their cells. They walked them through the long corridors and led them to a big hall. There the boys waited on their feet for a long time. In the dark. That's when your brother started to sing."

"Okay, that's enough now!" Mrs. Parvin dropped her spoon.

"No, it's not enough. There's a lot more," Mr. Parvin said and continued. "Do you know what he sang? 'From the blood of our youth, tulips are growing, tulips are growing, tulips are growing...'" He raised his voice, singing off tune.

Bibi rushed to the bathroom; everybody heard her sobbing violently, coughing, then throwing up. Her sister followed her.

"Sit down now," Mrs. Parvin said. "You ruined the dinner. Eat!"

"But I haven't told the rest of the story."
"No one wants to hear it. It's all in your head. No one was there to know how it happened."
"I have a source there. I trust him." He said this and immediately regretted it. He shouldn't have said anything about the bricklayer.
Everybody left the table. He could hear them arguing in the other room. At first it was a quarrel between the mother and the girls. Then they started to shout at each other. The girls blamed their mother for withholding the information about their father and brother, not letting them know what really happened. Then something broke. The little girl cried and rushed to the kitchen where Mr. Parvin sat alone against the dark window. He called her for the first time, asking her name.
"Do you know me?"
"You're Grandpa," the girl said, still crying, rubbing her eyes.
"And who are you?"
"I'm Sharah."
"Sharah or Sarah?"
"Sharah," the girl said strongly.
"Can I call you Shahrzad?"
"Okay."
Sharah's father came and took her to bed. Mr. Parvin stepped out on the porch. Holding his

right hand to the wall, he descended the steps down to the dark yard. He sat on the last step for a long time with Gorgi lying down at his side. He didn't talk to the dog, but listened to his breathing, smelled his woolen smell, felt his warmth. It was too dark to see anything, but he could feel the pansies dropping their heads, giving out a faint sweet scent.

There was a family meeting late that night. Mr. Parvin's son-in-law was trying to find a "logical solution" for everything. The old man could hear them from behind the wall. Although they had given him a pill, he couldn't sleep. He could hear the black neighbor, too. Down in his yard he moved the old bathtub, making a scraping sound.

"I've made an appointment for his eyes," Mr. Parvin's son-in-law was saying. "After the surgery, the house will be ready, too."

"You may fix his eyes, but what about his brain? He's gone insane!" Mrs. Parvin said and wept.

"He is not insane, Maman. We have to let him talk. Why do you shut him up?" One of the girls asked.

Mr. Parvin heard his wife answering and the sisters talking back at the same time. Things became confused again. Out of control. They raised their voices and the little girl burst into tears. Mr. Parvin pulled the blanket over his head not to hear all this. But he heard the bedroom door bang. His wife entered. He pretended to be asleep and from the edge of the blanket he saw her standing before the bathroom mirror, wiping her tears. She was tall and skeletal and a bit stooped, as if starting to lose bone tissue. Mr. Parvin remembered his wife's youth, when she was a beauty. She never wore high heels, so as not to look awkward walking with her shorter husband. Now she was crying in front of the mirror. This was her old habit. Mr. Parvin remembered her crying before many mirrors when she was young. She'd cry whenever something would go wrong. Then their daughters became crybabies too, and now little Sharah was crying her lungs out in the other room.

"Cry, cry! Let's all cry!" Mr. Parvin threw aside the blanket and sat up. His long white hair was disheveled. His pajama buttons were undone, showing his old red skin creased on his neck and chest like the spongy skin of a rooster's wattle. One of the twins ran in, sat on the bed and hugged her father tightly. She wept on his shoulder. This was Bibi, the dramatic one. Abi, carrying her crying girl in her arms, rushed to the bathroom to embrace her weeping mother. The son-in-law stood in the frame of the door, watching the Parvin family. He wiped his tears.

Down in the neighbor's yard, the black man pulled his broken chair close to the bathtub, sat there as if sitting by a pool, and opened a can of beer. He sang a sailor's song with an accent Mr. Parvin could not understand. But the song was so sad that it made the old man weep in his daughter's arms.

"Where is this place you're living, huh? Is this really America or is your husband poor?"

"I don't have a husband, Baba. This is Abi's house. I'm just staying here temporarily."

"Is your sister poor?"

"This is the only place we could afford, Baba," the son-in-law said from the frame of the door. "I'm an engineer, but I'm making keys in the corner of a grocery store. We've been trying to save some money—to move to a better neighborhood. But now we have to think about your home, sir. This is our priority."

"Home," Mr. Parvin said and sighed.

The next day, sitting on the last step of the porch, in front of the pansies and next to Gorgi, and now Sharah on his lap, Mr. Parvin told the bricklayer about last night. The bricklayer repeated the word "surgery" several times.

"Why do you repeat this word, my friend?

You don't mean to tell me..."

"It's all up to you, sir. See if you can avoid the surgery. But if you can't, then I may be able to come, or I may not. It's going to be harder. Much harder."

"I want your company, bricklayer. And it's not just because you bring me news. I like you, my friend. You're wise."

"I have to go now. There is a wall I have to finish back home."

"May I ask whose house you're building?"

"It's a new penitentiary, sir. I'm raising the walls."

"What an awful job, bricklayer. Couldn't you say no?"

"If I'd say no, they'd put me inside the walls."

"I understand."

For a few days Mr. Parvin couldn't call the bricklayer. It rained day and night, the basement flooded, and he heard his son-in-law walking with rubber boots knee-deep in the water, trying to sweep the flood out. The old man sat most of the day by the kitchen window, watching the gate. Gorgi was in the flooded basement. Mr. Parvin wondered how the poor dog could lie down. He thought about the surgery and what the bricklayer had told him. "See if you can avoid it." How could he avoid it? They would take him by force. He fantasized about escaping, going somewhere his family couldn't find him. He daydreamed about a sunny place, where he could remove the eye patch and call his friend.

It rained and rained and rained. Mr. Parvin's wife ironed, cooked quietly, now and then glanced at their son's picture and sniffled. Bibi, the jobless twin, locked herself up with a migraine headache. Abi went to school with high rubber boots and a long rubber raincoat, returning later with wet grocery bags and the flood news. Sharah was in and out of the kitchen all day, hugging a bald doll, or licking on a lollypop. Sometimes she sat on her grandfather's lap. Mr. Parvin whispered in her ear, "Are you my Shahrzad?" She nodded. "Tell me a story then." Sharah shrugged her shoulders, left Mr. Parvin's lap and wandered through the house.

"Rain, rain, rain..," Mr. Parvin muttered, and vaguely remembered the many sunny days back home when his children played in the yard and he watched them through the window, feeling proud of himself. He was a history teacher, wrote articles now and then, published here and there. But watching his children in the sun, he bragged to his scholar friends, "My best works, my masterpieces, are my children!"

Now a gust of wind opened the gate to the

yard and, as if the whole thing was a scene in a foggy, half-forgotten dream, Gorgi ran toward the gate and then out of the yard. He whispered, "Gorgi!" but no one heard him. Since his last speech at the dinner table he hadn't talked much and it was hard for him to make the effort. With difficulty he rose from his chair. Placing his hand on the tables and chairs, the walls and doorknobs, he dragged himself into the room where his wife was ironing sheets and pillowcases. He whispered, "Gorgi..," but his wife wasn't paying attention.

Mr. Parvin heard the squeaky elevator. His son-in-law came up all wet, water dripping from his hair and eyeglasses. The old man said, "Gorgi!" several times, motioning to the gate. His son-in-law rushed back inside the elevator and down to the yard.

"My head! My head is bursting! Please don't run that damned elevator!" Bibi banged her head on the wall. She was sitting on a cot, wearing a black scarf around her forehead and eyes like a pirate.

Which of my daughters are you? he wanted to ask. But he didn't, or couldn't. He guessed this must be the homeless one, the jobless one, the one without a husband. He tried to remember who her husband was and what had happened to him, but he couldn't concentrate. Limping to the bathroom, he closed the door and turned the lights on. There were eight bulbs around the mirror, he stared at them and removed the eye patch. Light poured inside his head. Closing his good eye tightly, he looked at the colorful shapes. He blinked; the shapes changed their forms and became something else. Now from behind the red and purple diamonds the bricklayer appeared. First as a midget, then taller, and finally the size of a tall man. Mr. Parvin closed the toilet lid, motioning to him to sit down.

"Sorry, friend. We can't go out. Sit on this. My wife has cleaned it. How are you?"

"As good as I can be."

"Something wrong?"

"The same."

"How is the wall?"

"The wall is rising. I'm working on it."

Mr. Parvin sighed and said nothing.

The bricklayer, who looked very gloomy today, rubbed his face as if he was tired. "When is your surgery?" he asked in a matter-of-fact way.

"The surgery? Oh, the eye surgery. One of these days. Should I be worried?"

"They're going to sew up your retina. You'll be able to see with your right eye."

"No colors and shapes?"

"No."

"And you?"

"It all depends. Let's see. Now I must go." The bricklayer stood up and stretched his long body, peering out the window. "A nasty place, isn't it? Look at your neighbor down there. His umbrella is full of holes. Is he crazy?"

"He is not the only crazy one around here, my friend. I'll see you on the first sunny day. Bye."

Turning the lights out, Mr. Parvin stepped into the bedroom. His wife sat on the edge of the bed, staring at the bathroom door. Her eyes were wet.

"I... was washing my hands," he mumbled.

"I know. Come, let me comb your hair."

She sat him at the dressing table, combed his thick, white hair. She always did this gently and tenderly as if she was still in love with him. She ran the comb through his hair slowly, taking her time, prolonging it. She didn't put anything on her husband's hair. She liked the soft, silky feel of it.

"Did you hear me in the bathroom?" Mr. Parvin asked guiltily.

"No, dear, I didn't," she said in a whisper.

Mr. Parvin's son-in-law didn't come until eleven that night. His dinner grew cold. His wife walked back and forth restlessly, chewing her nails. Sharah burst into tears every fifteen minutes.

Pressing his forehead against the cold windowpane, Mr. Parvin curved his hands around his face to see the dark yard. Finally his son-in-law entered the open gate, dragging a heavy sack on the ground. The twins put on their identical raincoats made of shiny yellow rubber and rushed to the yard. Mr. Parvin saw them taking Gorgi's corpse out of the burlap sack. Now the neighbor appeared with a shovel. It was pouring as if the sky were a sea upsidedown. Mr. Parvin had to make an effort to see what they were doing.

  The whole thing was like the fragments of a dream. The black man digging a grave along the wall of the yard, Mr. Parvin's daughters and his son-in-law lifting the heavy carcass, dumping it in the hole, burying the dog. In a minute they came up in the doorless elevator, muddy from head to foot, bringing the black man with them into the kitchen. The girls sobbed, blowing their noses. Gorgi had been their companion since their first days in America. The neighbor said something no one understood. He shook his head in regret. The son-in-law opened a can of beer for him. Mrs. Parvin fed him warm soup.

It rained for one more week and when they sat at the kitchen table or in the living room they heard the tides of the flood water hitting the walls of the basement. Mr. Parvin's son-in-law gave up on sweeping out the rain water. He sat all day, pulling the prickly hairs of his thick moustache, thinking about a logical solution for all this mess. The schools were closed. Abi, the teacher, didn't go out anymore. The twins sat in front of the silent TV, watching the maps and charts of the weather channel. Most of the week Mr. Parvin limped the length of the house from one window to another, waiting for the rain to stop. Now standing for a few seconds at the bedroom window, the black neighbor raised his head up, waving to him. Mr. Parvin waved back. The neighbor sat on a broken chair by his overflowing bathtub, holding a crooked umbrella over his head, drinking a beer.

On the first dry day, Mrs. Parvin combed her husband's hair back and splashed some cologne on his face. She wore her good dress, the black crepe skirt and jacket she came to this country in. She put some lipstick on. The daughters dressed up and little Sharah wore a big pink bow on top of her red curls. They all crammed into Abi's small Toyota to take Mr. Parvin to the hospital. Although the sun was not out and it was a cold day, they felt a vague joy.

Sitting by the window next to his wife, Mr. Parvin turned his head toward the street and removed his eye patch. He shut his good eye. The car moved fast, the images from the kaleidoscope whirled, turned, and changed shape rapidly. Mr. Parvin saw the bricklayer approaching from the margin of the freeway. The old man motioned to him to stop. The bricklayer shouldn't enter the car. They couldn't talk now. But it was too late. Mr. Parvin's friend was already sitting in the front seat, managing to fit himself between Sharah and her mother. He turned back to look at Mr. Parvin.

"The surgery, huh?"

Mr. Parvin nodded.

"I just came to say don't worry. I'll be around."

Mr. Parvin smiled and pulled the eye patch down over his eye.

This was the first happy meal in a long time. The whole family sat around Mr. Parvin's bed in the small hospital room. Sharah sat at her grandfather's feet. Mr. Parvin leaned against the pillows with a thick bandage around his head. Everybody was biting into fat sandwiches, the thick mayonnaise dripping on their hands and wrists. The twins talked at the same time with full mouths. The jobless Bibi was reporting about the possibility of a new job in an Italian restaurant. The owner had told her she looked Italian, she could pretend to be one. The son-in-law was saying that the house was almost ready. Mr. and Mrs. Parvin could move in within a week.

Mr. Parvin didn't finish his sandwich. When they asked him why he wasn't eating, he said he was keeping a few bites for Gorgi. The girls looked at each other and burst into tears. Sharah cried too, spilling her soda on the hospital blanket. The family ate the rest of their food in silence. When they all left, Mr. Parvin looked at the window and saw the clean blue sky and the top of a white tower. He touched his bandage. He was tempted to remove it, but he didn't. He feared blood and pain. He closed his open eye, tried to see the image of the bricklayer in the darkness of his head. He saw it for a second, but then the image blurred and disappeared. This was seeing him with his mind's eye. Mr. Parvin wanted the real man.

Mr. Parvin spent most of that night watching the top of the white tower swimming in the dark sky. He wondered who lived there.

When they removed Mr. Parvin's bandages, Sharah screamed, "Grandpa has two eyes!" Everybody laughed.

Leaving the hospital, Mr. Parvin looked at the white tower for the last time. He wanted to know where that place was, but he didn't ask. Now both of his eyes were open. He had to wear a dark shade to protect the sensitive eye. No kaleidoscope, no diamonds and circles. In the car, he looked silently at the fast-passing street scenes. His son-in-law took them to see the new house.

"This is beautiful!" the girls laughed, running in the empty house. Sharah, overjoyed, hollered and screamed. Her voice echoed in the empty rooms. Mr. Parvin's son-in-law walked him from one room to another, showing him the house. A very old house with fresh paint. A better neighborhood than theirs. A yard, an oak tree, green grass, and a bench facing two identical crepe myrtles, now dry, but promising to bloom in the spring. Mrs. Parvin opened all the kitchen cabinets; she pulled all the drawers out.

The Parvins moved in a few days later. Not much to bring with them. They took some of Abi's furniture, intending to buy more in the future. Bibi moved in with them and started the restaurant job. Mrs. Parvin and her son-in-law took Mr. Parvin to another doctor, a psychiatrist. He wrote a prescription for Mr. Parvin's depression and occasional hallucinations. Then his son-in-law took him to a barbershop to cut his now very long hair. Having so many chores to do in their new house, Mrs. Parvin didn't have time to wash and comb her husband's hair.

On the barber's raised chair, Mr. Parvin sat staring at himself with both eyes. The barber talked and clipped his silky hair. Feeling the old man's bump under his fingers, he asked what that little walnut was? Mr. Parvin's son-in-law explained that when his father-in-law was a small naughty boy, he fell out of a tree and that's how the bump grew there. Mr. Parvin either didn't understand the conversation or paid no attention to it. He was immersed in a scene he was watching in the barber's mirror. Through the open door of the shop he saw a half-built structure across the street. A worker stood on a scaffold laying bricks on top of bricks. Mr. Parvin watched him and waited patiently until the end of the haircut. When they left the shop, he turned toward the building, raised his head and looked up. The worker turned to see him. The strong sun was in his eyes. He held his broad hand over his brow and gazed at Mr. Parvin for a long second. As if finally recognizing the old man, he smiled. The creases of his sunburnt forehead opened, and his white teeth gleamed in the noon light. Mr. Parvin smiled back and winked at the worker, feeling a tickling joy he hadn't felt for a long time. Knowing now that the bricklayer would always be around, he let his son-in-law take him home.

CROSSING

With that lost and desperate look, that restless look which holds a deep sea of sadness at its bottom, he watches me in the mirror. The rubber belt is running under my feet. I'm walking at the speed of 4:00, incline of 3:00, toward nowhere, to reach nothing. I'm walking in one spot for my health. I look at my tormented face in the mirror and that's when I see him watching me. I try not to look at him. I busy myself reading the red, flashing digits displayed on the machine. I raise the incline to 5:00, the speed to 4:50. I almost run on this moving hill, gasping, sweating my life out, to avoid his eyes.

There is something very familiar about this man—his pleading look, as if asking for help, his fatigued, hunched way of sitting on the press bench, something you don't see in this place, the way he rests his large fists under his chin. I rub my eyes to make sure I haven't made a mistake. I look at his black hair, parted by a distinct line, combed to one side, oiled and glistening like a raven's feathers. He keeps watching me.

I remember when he was thirty-five and I was eight. Crossing to the other side of busy streets, he held my hand tightly in his. He had big warm hands, even hot, almost burning at times.

I look at the man's hands. He notices my glance, takes them from under his chin and lays them limply on his lap.

One, two, three, four... fifty-four, seventy-four... I've belted myself tightly to this instrument called the abdominal chair, bending and unbending one hundred times. Each time I raise my torso, a gray-haired man appears in front of me, sitting on a bicycle, but not pedaling. He just watches me. This is a different man, but he has borrowed the same sad eyes. A faint, barely visible smile, a kind of smile that only I can tell is a smile, stretches the right corner of his mouth; his eyes are dark, black waters at the bottom of a well. He is hypnotizing me, piercing me.

The gray-haired man's lips are sealed as they were in those years. The years that he talked less and looked lost. He was in his fifties when I was away and received his pictures. In these pictures, his hair is parted by a line and laid to one side, not raven's feathers anymore, but ashes, soft and powdery, sitting lightly on his head, waiting for a wind to blow them away. How many of these pictures did I receive when I was away? And now, sitting on this idle bike, he is staring at me. Ninety-four, ninety-five, one hundred. Done with the abdominal.

Now he plays tricks on me, as in the last years, after his stroke, when some of his brain's wiring had burned or half-burned and he became a different man. Sitting on the arm extension bench, he stares at me from behind his dark sunglasses, pretending to be blind. I'm climbing these stairs up to nowhere, to reach nothing, to ascend while I remain in the same spot, just for my health. These are the endless steps of an imaginary tower, the steps of a nightmare, in which I climb and climb and end up where I've started.

Now he tries to amuse me. He sits on the arm extension bench, watching me through his dark glasses, smiling faintly. He makes faces, sticks his tongue out, blows his cheeks, trying to make me laugh. His hair is snow white—not even one black strand is left. Is he really blind? In both eyes?

In his last years, after the stroke, his left eye went blind and many fuses blew in his left hemisphere. He lost interest in everything. He stopped loving. The loving wire had burned out, too. When I saw him after many years, years of just looking at his pictures, he didn't open his arms to me, didn't say a kind word. All he said was "I can't see well! Where am I?"

And even when he remembered me, when I repeated to him that it was I, nothing changed. I said I was the one he loved, the one he lost, the one he wrote to, the one he sent the bad news to—the news of the executions, the common grave where they dumped the bloody corpses... I said I was the one who aged here, while he aged there. I was the one who carried his love like sharp shards in my heart. And finally, when I convinced him that I was the same one who had learned from him how to live, he still acted as if I were just a distant acquaintance, or a hired nurse. He complained about his eye patch sliding down, and his good eye going bad.

"I can't see well," he moaned. "The lights bother me," he whined. "Cover both of my eyes. I don't want to see!" he ordered.

And now his eyes are covered with these thick, dark lenses. I'm climbing the steps; I've burnt one hundred fifty calories. It's twenty minutes now that I've been climbing, and there are more steps to go; the goal is to burn two hundred fifty calories. He stares at me, I at him. Squeak, squeak, squeak, the machine cries under my tired feet. He gets up, and limps blindly through the wheels, chairs, benches, and weights, finding his way out among thick-muscled men and women. I try to follow him, but I lose him in the crowd of greasy, flexing biceps and triceps.

In the women's locker room, I change into my bathing suit, open the opaque glass door, and enter the whirlpool area. I shower, and step into the steaming pool. He is here again; he has somehow sneaked into the women's whirlpool. As old as a hundred-year-old, as withered and rotten as an ancient water lily on the muddy waters of a forgotten pond, he has spread his gray arms and is floating, his white petals, separating from their blossoms, wrinkling on the surface of the water as if dissolving. He dies before my eyes. A trembling smile rests on his mouth, as if a song will soon reach his open lips.

I sink in the hot water and wait for his voice. I wait for his sad song to tell me the story of the prince who cut off the flesh of his thigh to feed his flying horse. But there is no voice.

He dies before my eyes just as he did on the hospital bed. The transparent tubes carried his blood out of his head into four jars the size and shape of pickle jars, sitting in a row on the floor against the wall. I watched his skin turning gray, a color I had never seen on a human being. His lips trembled as now and I waited for the voice to emerge. And it didn't. Not even a sigh. All I had of him at that moment was his left wrist, pulsing into my palm. I tried to absorb his last pulse, taking the remains of his life into mine, to preserve him, here, in the chambers of my heart.

Now I pass through the wall of glistening flesh and sweating muscles. The wall of life. Drumming sounds of raised heart rates follow me, Boom-boom, boom-boom, fading behind me as I step into the cool night. My skin steams here and sweat beads dry on my temples. I stand among the passers-by, bewildered and lost, looking around for him. The street before me floods like a river; I don't dare to cross alone. I need his large, burning hand to hold mine, to help me pass to the other side.

THE PILLAR
For Turaj

Like a voice from childhood, far away and inaccessible, he calls out something in the language of dreams, painful and alien. A dry sob, a tearless cry. He is the one sitting on the cement, the foundation of this human tower, he is the bearer of the burden, the one below.

But even he can sleep and dream.

I'm the one on the top tonight, the privileged, the head of the tower, the one close to the eye-window of the ceiling, the one who can trace the clouds at twilight, measuring the turquoise against the sapphire. I'm the one who can think.

Sitting on each other's shoulders, we take turns being the one on the top, the one who has no burden, who can sleep.

The cell is square, three by four meters, good for five prisoners to sleep side by side. We were ten once. We slept horizontally, sardines in a can. They added ten more. Now the only way to sleep is to make human towers.

It's my turn tonight. I sit on someone's shoulder, he is on someone else's, the third is on the fourth, and the fifth one is the foundation, sitting on the cement, a mountain balancing on his back. Last night I was at the bottom, now it's my turn to rest. But the position is shaky. If I sneeze or scratch my head the whole tower wobbles, the four people under me may lose their balance. We are sitting against the wall; I try to lean back and close my eyes. But sleep does not come.

Up here I'm the king. We call the one on top the king. I've divided my reign into three periods. I don't need to sleep the whole six hours. For the first two hours I watch the sky. It's summer and the blackout happens when the sky is still bright. I sit here, witnessing the moment-to-moment change of the colors. Sometimes a tinge of orange lingers, melting into the lavender. Sometimes a lost bird flies in confusion. Once I saw the rainbow.

For an hour I count sheep. I envision a stream, the sheep—wooly, white, and fat, their loose tails hanging over their buttocks—jump clumsily over the stream. One sheep... two sheep... three... four... until I reach three-digit numbers. Now I'm confused; I lose count and open my eyes. For the next two hours I fight with anger, anger at myself for wasting my sleeping time. Then I give up and sit alert, waiting for the red glow of the dawn. My eyes are wide open, sand dry, tearless, awake. I descend.

During the day, when the guards take some of us out for interrogation, we remain in a perpetual sitting position, knees pressed to chests. We leave a small circle in the middle of the cell for movement. In groups of five, we trudge around the circle. To the right, then to the left. If someone looks at this view from above, he'll see a wheel turning, going nowhere. We stop three times: for lunch, dinner, and toilet before sleep. We barely talk.

We don't like each other. We're all here as the result of pursuing a common goal, but since our routes were different, we are not comrades. Our pursuit is as absurd as trying to reach the city of X, one walking on foot, one riding on a horse, one traveling with a group, one carrying a weapon, one praying while traveling, one holding a flag and a banner, all seeking the same city but hating each other for using different means to get there. All arrested for moving toward X, but now despising each other.

So we sit in silence or walk around a circle, to the right and to the left. As the days pass in a constant but immobile struggle for our necessities, we forget the cause, the reasons for it, and the logic to all of this.

Up here I can think sometimes. If it is possible in this cell to think at all, it's every four days, sitting up here on the pillar of four other sets of shoulders, next to the eye-window. I think while watching the sky changing colors; I think while counting the fat sheep; I think in anger, when I get close to the end of my reign; I think at dawn.

There is seldom any disturbance through the night, but now this voice, this childhood voice, his or mine, remote and inaccessible, calls out in a dream language. Now this dry sob disturbs my thoughts. I'm not sure who is under us tonight, bearing the burden of four men on his shoulders. I do not know his name. I listen to him all night, pulling in my belly muscles to weigh less. Maybe his back is breaking under the burden.

But I envy him and his nightmares. He is sleeping; I'm not.

Woe to me, the listener of my cellmates' cries: a king not, a priest rather, hearing confessions in a dream language from below. The bearer of my cellmates' fears, the owl, the owner of images of a million fat sheep, an ex-traveler to the city of X, weaponless, on foot, blindly following the trail of leaders in a dense fog. Woe to me, sleepless at the bottom, in the middle, and on top. A useless burden on human shoulders, shortly a bearer of human weight.

ALI THE LITTLE
(Tehran, Iran, 1980)

From the end of the narrow alley, where the bakery is, Ali the Little yo-yos all the way home, carrying in his left hand a tall, hot Barbari bread almost his own height. Ali is seven, but he is as small as a four-year-old. He is nicknamed Ali the Little not only because he is short, but because there is an Ali the Big living down the street who is twelve years old, a bully, and beats the other boys up.

Under the arrows of flashing rockets zooming across the evening sky, Ali presses himself to the graffiti on the wall, which curse the West, the East, the infidels and the leftists. He walks under the eaves of the houses, as if they can protect him from the bombs, or he yo-yos inside and around the thick column of search light, looking up to find its hidden source. In the heat, in the cold, in wartime, and peace, Ali the Little yo-yos and carries that long Barbari bread home.

Ali's father is our first-floor neighbor. He's called Haj-Agha, or Haji, but no one is sure if he has really been to Mecca for pilgrimage or he just calls himself Haji because he wishes to be one, or he thinks he looks like one. Ali's father is fat and tall and has a greasy, fleshy face always covered with two days growth of gray, prickly beard. He works in the neighborhood mosque, manages the food coupons and heads the vigilante groups who police the streets and arrest whoever looks suspicious. Haji is on the mosque's payroll now, but no one knows what his job was before the revolution, before moving to this neighborhood, where there were no real or fake Hajis within ten kilometers.

This alley is in Keshavarz Boulevard (Queen Elizabeth Boulevard before the revolution); it is a clean middle-class neighborhood, with not too fancy, not too shabby apartments, right next to Tulip Park. But our apartment building and the building on our right are old, dark, and ugly. Maybe when the landlord built these two buildings twenty years ago, there were not so many tall houses around to block the light. Now our southern windows open to the brick walls of the houses of the alley that runs parallel to ours, and the windows to the north are almost blocked by a massive mansion another Haji (a real one, for sure) has been trying to build for months. If it happens that we're home in the morning, we notice that a huge fifty-story high-rise in the northeast blocks the sun's rays until one in the afternoon. Condominiums in this high-rise had been bought by the affluent before the revolution, but now are occupied by the families of the militia and the revolutionary guards. Haji must have arrived late, otherwise he'd have been living in one of these luxury condos.

Ali and his family live on the first floor of our dark apartment building, an old man by the name of Amu and his numerous family members live on the second floor, and we live on the third. Amu must be some kind of relative of Haji. Haji probably brought him and his family from their village. They all have a thick accent, they all pray many times a day, and they're all involved in Haji's mosque activity. The women on the second floor make black flags for the mourning processions and demonstrations from dawn to night. Their old sewing machines clatter and rattle, stitching the flags' hems.

Ali the Little is the only member of this big tribe who says hi or bye to us. Whenever he sees me in the alley, holding Nima's hand, teaching him patiently how to walk, he stops yo-yoing and strokes my baby's head, lifts him up in the air and talks baby talk with him. Once he even saved his small allowance and bought a fat, yellow yo-yo for Nima, not knowing that a one-year-old has a long way to go before he can play with a yo-yo. I thanked Ali and kissed him on his cheeks, but immediately looked around to see if anyone had seen me. Who knows? Maybe they'd arrest me for kissing a seven-year-old boy.

So Ali the Little is fond of my little boy, and, who knows, maybe he is fond of me too, because I look so different from his mother and those flag-maker relatives hidden under the tent of their black veils. But if, by chance, Haj-Agha comes to the door and sees Ali talking to us, he calls him inside and we hear him scolding the boy, shoving him into the room. The next day, again, on the way to school, or on the way back with his long Barbari bread in one hand, the yo-yo in the other, Ali stops to talk to me and plays with Nima.

Ali the Little is a sweet boy and in spite of his sour father all the neighborhood loves him. Ali's mother lives inside her black veil and is seldom seen. She is either somewhere in the dark kitchen cooking for Haji, or squatting on the floor of the toilet, clawing the dirty laundry. When the second-floor neighbors, tired of sewing black flags of the martyrs, take a long nap in the afternoon, we hear Ali the Little's mother humming something to herself with a voice that is thin and sad. When Haji comes home she shuts up. Most of the time the hubbub of voices of so many men and women living in Amu's house, or the monotonous prayer chant coming from their radio (loud on purpose, for the whole block to hear), prevents us from hearing the sounds of Haji's house, except when Haji is mad and raises his voice so high that it covers even the Friday Prayer. When this happens the flag makers and their men instantly quiet themselves so that they can eavesdrop.

Haji becomes mad exactly once a week, every Thursday evening at seven o'clock, right before the muezzin climbs the mosque's tall minaret and announces the evening prayer. First he quarrels with his wife, then he shouts at Ali, his voice rising gradually, until his curses become completely audible, not only to us, but to the neighbors on our right and left too.

"You son of a bitch! You little mischievous devil! I'll teach you a good lesson, bastard—." Then we hear an even, repetitive sound, something like *swish... swish... swish..*, and Ali's mother wails.

Haj-Agha's hostility toward us continues for a long time. It's quite understandable. We never pray, never get near the mosque, I don't wear a scarf, and every night at least a dozen young people come to our house, sometimes parking their motorcycles out front. Seeing us in the stairway, Haji drops his head as if he hasn't seen us. Seeing our friends entering the building, he goes into his apartment, banging the door on himself. Hearing our music, he sends Ali upstairs to tell us to turn it down, he is praying. He has influenced Amu and his family too. They've become hostile as well. Not that they've ever been friendly, but at least when we'd say hello, they'd hello back, or the wife and the other women, who are either daughters and daughters-in-law or additional wives, would raise their heads from their black flags, smile at Nima, or tell him something pleasant in their native tongue.

The door of Amu's apartment is always wide open and all these women sit on the floor of the hallway, sewing flags, their men eating something—watermelon with bread and cheese, or greasy beef stew. Each time we climb the steps to our home we have to face the open steaming mouth of their apartment. Now that they are under Haji's influence they all resent us and a dozen pairs of eyes gaze at us as if we're from the planet Mars. No hi, no bye.

One evening when we have twenty people upstairs, celebrating Nima's first birthday, Haji and Amu knock on the door. Afshin, my husband, recognizes their fat shadows behind the opaque glass door, rushes to the living room and motions to our friends to hide the beer and vodka bottles. Mehran and Fariba are the ones who make homemade beer and vodka; they bottle and bring them to parties. Haji and Amu keep knocking until the table is clear of liquor. All the bottles are in the kitchen sink and five women have made a wall around it, pretending they're washing the dishes. Now Afshin opens the door and Asef, our sweet talker, stands behind him, ready to use diplomacy, if necessary.

"We have to check the gas pipes," Haji says, "Downstairs gas is leaking—" He pushes the door open and Amu follows him. Since the heaters are all connected to gas pipes, checking the pipes means roaming every room of the house. As Haj-Agha and the old man walk from one room to another, saying "Ya Allah!" to warn the women about their male presence, Asef distracts them with his non-stop chattering about the latest war news, the explosion of a government building down the street, and the Ayatollah who was martyred a few days ago. Then he asks several questions about Haji's mosque and its revolutionary activities. Surrounded by Asef, Afshin, and a couple of other friends, who follow them from room to room, the intruders can't see much around them. There are of course plenty of forbidden books and magazines, forbidden food and drinks in every corner of the house, and the women are all wearing forbidden clothes. But Haj-Agha and Amu are politely pushed out of the apartment after making sure that all the pipes are safe. Before closing the door on them, Asef offers them a piece of birthday cake, which they reject.

One day, almost a month after the birthday party, Haj-Agha's wife opens her apartment door just in time to find me on the landing. Her mission is to spy on me, to see when I leave and with whom I come back, who is my baby sitter today, and why my grandmother hasn't visited me lately. Now she catches me in the landing and says,
"Haji wants to see you tonight."
"Me?"
"Aha ... You're a teacher, aren't you?"
I nod.
"He wants you to teach English to Ali."
"But I teach at the university. I don't have much experience with kids."
"That's all right. If you teach grown-ups, you can teach the kids as well. Haji wants Ali to learn English."
I bring this up at dinner. A few friends are eating with us. They all believe that Haj-Agha is puzzled about us and our life-style, and by hiring me as a teacher he can try to figure us out. Militias and vigilantes are gaining power in all the neighborhoods, Asef says, I'd better go and tutor the boy if I don't want trouble. We'd better not confront these people, my husband says.

It's a Wednesday night. I take Nima with me downstairs and he cheers and laughs when he sees Ali the Little—his older small friend who's only a bit taller than himself. Ali and Nima play on the freshly swept carpet; they roll and laugh. It's amazing how Ali enjoys the company of my one-year-old. I sit on the floor under the picture of the frowning Imam Khomeini, pulling my skirt down on my legs, making sure no skin shows. But I'm still not wearing a scarf. (I resist wearing it until it becomes mandatory and the vigilantes beat women up in the streets if they walk with their hair uncovered).

Haji comes in saying "Ya Allah," and sits as far from me as he can possibly manage, gazing at the white wall, away from me. He says that he understands that I've studied in America and I'm a teacher. He wants me to teach English to Ali. I agree to go twice a week, Mondays and Wednesdays at nine. He doesn't talk about a salary and I don't say anything. The whole thing sounds like an order, but I don't mind much because I like Ali the Little. Then the woman offers me a glass of dark tea and Haji asks me questions. What is my husband's job? Where are our parents, and where are we originally from? At the end he asks if I'm a Christian. I say no.

"A Jew, then?"

"No, sir."
"You're not a Zoroastrian?"
"No, sir."
He pauses for a few minutes, hesitating to ask more. There is only one religion left and that's Baha'i. Bahaists are being arrested and executed every day, because of their prophet's "revision" of Islam.
"My family on both sides are Moslems," I tell him.
"And yourself?"
"I believe in God."
"But not practicing?"
"No, sir."
He gets up and leaves the room. The wife leaves too. I sit for a moment alone, watching Ali and Nima playing quietly with toy cars, Ali making low, whistling, bomb sounds with his mouth, hitting the cars, Nima laughing. Then the woman comes in with a thin notebook and a pencil for Ali and tells him to stop playing, it's class time. Ali wants to play, but his mother says if he doesn't stop playing this minute his father will punish him.
I teach ABCD to Ali, half way to L, and I stop.

The following Monday, a few minutes before

nine, Ali comes up and knocks on our door. He hands me a folded fabric.

"My mother said please wear this when you come down. My father is home."

I unfold the fabric. It's a large, black head scarf, almost the size of a tablecloth.

In this way a few months pass. I tutor Ali the Little every Monday and Wednesday and I don't wear the black scarf. Haj-Agha never shows up again, but his wife offers me hot tea after each session, and interrogates me, asking questions that are obviously not hers. What do I think about the war? Did I vote last week or not? Are Asef and other boys who come to our house our cousins, or just friends?

The war escalates; a nearby neighborhood is hit by a bomb; a dozen people are buried alive. Haji is busy. He and his boys, the bearded vigilantes, guard the streets day and night. The food lines are longer now, coupons are bought and sold on the black market by the guards themselves, the head scarf becomes mandatory, a few ayatollahs are assassinated, and Amu's black flags are planted on top of all the buildings. Every other day is a martyr's day and streets change names overnight. The martyr who was more important wipes out the name of his predecessor from the street sign. Prayer chants echo in the depth of the night. The whole country has turned into a massive mosque. This is when the university fires me for not filling out the ideological questionnaire.

One day they cancel all the classes and call the faculty to the office. A bearded man from the Ministry of Islamic Guidance, formerly the Ministry of Culture, speaks for a few minutes about the "Cultural Revolution" and then they put us all—a dozen literature and drama professors—in a mini-bus and take us to the former Rudaki Hall. Our magnificent Opera Hall is now a mass prayer center.

The big lobby is empty of the velvet furniture, but the huge chandelier still hangs above our heads. Someone from the Ministry orders everyone to sit on the marble floor. Professors of the Arts and Humanities from all of the universities are present. We all sit on the cold marble and veiled women pass several different forms out. We have to fill them out, then go to another room to be interviewed. These are ideological questions. What is your religion? If you say Islam, then there are detailed questions about the rules and regulations and rituals. One question demands the whole text of a prayer in Arabic. Obviously all these sheets remain blank. Not only my parents but my grandparents never prayed or attended a mosque. Almost half of the professors get up after a few minutes. I glance at Afshin, Asef, and other friends in the men's section; they're getting up. I rise and we all leave quietly. We know that we shouldn't go back to our classrooms.

The official letters indicating that we're not ideologically qualified to teach come in few days.

This was in March. One April afternoon Fariba and her husband Mehran and then Asef come up to our apartment to tell us that a massive arrest has begun. It is a countdown, they say. Everybody is hiding. I pack Nima's things: a few diapers, one tin box of formula—all we could get with our last coupon—and the yellow yo-yo, Ali the Little's gift. This is a Thursday evening and Haji comes home early. We have to find a way to leave the building without being seen. We don't know our destination yet, but we know that we have to travel light, leaving everything behind. At the last moment I glance at the bookcase covering three walls of the living room. Most of these are English books we brought in boxes from the States, and then old Persian translations of world literature I've been collecting since I was a child. A few rare editions handed down to me by my grandfather. I glance at my old, leather-bound Hafiz, Rumi, Khayaam for the last time. Before leaving I squeeze my own manuscripts—stories, plays, and unfinished translations—into the knapsack next to the diapers.

On the first landing, we stop. Haji is shouting in his apartment and we have to make sure their door is not open. He curses someone and his voice rises as he gets angrier. There is a slap and someone falls on something. Then there is a loud bang. His wife moans and now the sound of *swish, swish, swish*—. We tiptoe down the steps. Amu's door is closed; no one is breathing inside. They must be listening to Haji's weekly show. On the last landing we hear the swish sound more loudly, it comes from behind the door; something hits the tiled floor. Then we hear a whimper, a whine, a small animal's thin, desperate voice from the bottom of a black, scary hole: "Don't, Father—don't! For the sake of Imam, don't! If you love Imam Khomeini, don't—"

Swish, swish, swish ... Haj-Agha whips the child, the mother sobs, and we close the door of our dark apartment forever, leaving Ali the Little behind.

ON THE ROOFTOP

Under her black veil, in the darkest fold, where the sharp odor of rose water mixes with the scent of earth and dust of many holy shrines, in a hidden corner, under her long, thick chador, death sits silently, brooding.

She knows he is here, but she ignores him and busies herself with the routines of her evening prayer. She does not pray for him to go, because if he is here, living under her chador, it's meant by God, it's His will and who is she to confront the Almighty? If he is here, sitting with that narrow body of his, with knees folded into his chest, breathing quietly, waiting for her to finish her day's chores, let him be. If her time has come, it has come.

So she doesn't pray for him to leave, she prays for her children, who are not with her anymore. The boy has been down there for the past ten years, in the courtyard, buried under the persimmon tree where he used to play as a child, and the girl is somewhere on the other side of the ocean, in a dark, faraway place, damper and lonelier than where her brother lives. She prays for the girl—who is alive—more than for the buried boy, because she thinks that the boy, who was killed and his corpse brought home one rainy day, is now in the sunny courtyard of his own house, but the girl, who left, is somewhere rainy, lonely and dark. She needs God's attention, she deserves a prayer more than her brother does, who lies in peace.

This way, thinking about them, seeing their faces in her mind, imagining them in their dark places, measuring their comfort and discomfort, as she has done all through her life, she spreads her cashmere cloth on the carpet, faces the diamond-shaped window and slowly unfolds her embroidered prayer kerchief, as if the sacred stone and the carnelian rosary are made of ether and will evaporate. She kisses the sura that is carved on the stone and lays the smooth rock gently on the kerchief next to the rosary. After arranging everything meticulously she pulls the black chador off her head and folds it in four. She does this slowly and gently, as if a butterfly is trapped inside the folds of the veil and she doesn't want to chase it away.

When she lays the folded fabric on the carpet a faint odor of camphor rises and this startles her. He's here waiting, she thinks, with that peculiar smell of his, but he's a patient boy, he won't rush. Now she picks up her white, transparent prayer veil and arranges it on her head, then looks out the diamond of the window, which has framed the courtyard. Under the heavy persimmon, now leafless but shining with glowing orange fruit, there is a rectangular flower bed, covered with purple pansies. That's where her son sleeps. She murmurs the words of the prayer absentmindedly and listens to the neighbor's children playing in the next yard. For a second she confuses time and place and feels the presence of her own children and thinks that they are chasing each other around the pool, shouting with excitement. When she comes to, she murmurs the words which meaning she's never learned, the words of the language of God, which are not hers but are sacred. She has memorized them and repeated them like a parrot since she was a child.

The real prayer for her is when the foreign words end and it's her turn to talk. And she talks with God the way she talks with her sister, Poori. God is her absent friend, her invisible companion, an intimate roommate, closer than her husband used to be in the first years of their marriage, closer than even her sister; God is her own self.

She talks to God as she talks to her image in the mirror and gazes outside until dusk descends. She stares at the darkening courtyard and says: "Well, God, you've sent for me and he's sitting here under my veil, waiting patiently. This must be my last talk with you, so I'm telling you that I'm ready to go. The boy is under the tree, inside your earth, and I'll tell my sister to keep decorating his little flower bed with pansies in the spring and autumn, marigolds in the summer and lilies in the freezing winter. I know that he is not up there with you, he's right here where he belongs and is resting in peace at last.

"But do you remember his restlessness? His riotous spirit? His sharp tongue? Remember how he wanted to change the world and fight with demons and restore justice, as he kept saying? What happened then? The devil took him, put him against the wall, your wall, God, and pierced him with hot bullets—your bullets. Because if you had not willed him to die, he wouldn't have died the way he did. You could at least have let him live a few more years, get married, and bring me a grandchild. Then this uninvited guest wouldn't crawl under my chador like a hissing snake, waiting for me to finish my chores. He'd know that there is another child to raise, he'd wait twenty more years. But it's all your will, God, and it's too late anyway; so I submit as I've always done and obey your orders.

"And the girl is in that remote land, which is dark most of the time, and it rains all day in spring and summer and snows the rest of the year. How can she be happy without the sun, God? Could you be happy without sunshine?

"You remember that after the guards brought her brother and we buried him together under this persimmon, the girl didn't stop sobbing for a long time. I heard her every night in her room, pressing her face to the pillow to muffle her cries. I sent her to this class and that class, because they wouldn't let her inside their universities, and she learned and half-learned a bit of this and a bit of that—language, drawing, sewing, and typing. But her night sobs wouldn't stop. One day, you're my witness, I called her and told her, 'Your uncle's daughter is going abroad to study; do you want to go with her? Your share of the inheritance, what your father left for you, is untouched, your brother's money is yours too. Take it and go. The house is good enough for me. I can always let the two rooms, take tenants in and manage my life. And you know that I like to be alone. Your Auntie Poori visits me every Friday like clockwork and spends the whole weekend with me, so I won't be that lonely and the neighbors are nice too. I've lived here for thirty years, for God's sake—people know me and care for me. Go, girl, go with your cousin and take that scarf off your pretty head. Let your hair breathe, dear, let the wind blow your sorrows away. Don't you know that I can hear

you every night, your head in the pillow, weeping and shaking like a willow?'
"So she leaves. I send her off and I'm relieved. And that's your will, God. If you hadn't put those words in my head, I could never have convinced the girl to go. She insisted for months. She said she should stay with me and take care of me. But I could see that a pair of candles burned in her eyes. Her eyes had a glow they didn't have before, and you know what that glow was.
"So she insisted for a while but didn't weep in her bed anymore. I called her uncle and talked to him and gave him the money and the money bought her freedom. Her uncle bribed whomever he needed to bribe, bought the girls' visas and passports and they left.
"Now why am I telling you all this? Didn't you arrange it yourself? Weren't you behind everything?"

In this way she murmurs and whispers and tells and retells stories that her God has already heard. Now she stops and collects her prayer stone and rosary, wraps them in the kerchief and wraps the kerchief in the square cashmere cloth and puts the bundle on the table. She takes the white prayer veil off and folds it in four, but she doesn't put on the black veil yet; she leaves it in the corner of the room in its dark folds, watching it for a second, noticing that it's throbbing faintly, as if a ghost breathes underneath.

There is a wooden box she keeps under her bed, she carries it to the living room and sets it next to the prayer bundle. She unlocks the box with a small golden key and opens it slowly as if it contains the ashes of burned memories and they'll blow away with the faintest breeze. But inside the box there are smaller boxes, something of the past hiding in each. The smallest of all is a tiny tin box containing three little teeth. The teeth belonged to her son, when he was six, and lost them to grow the new ones. The slightly bigger box contains her daughter's hair. When she was fourteen she cut her long hair for the first time to become fashionable. Now lifeless and dry, the dark braid coils like the fossil of a boa in the box. The third box contains her late husband's wedding band, cufflinks and tie pin. The large gold band still shines, but the silver cufflinks and the pin are tarnished. In the larger box there are a few letters. Her son sent them from prison, twice a year maybe, whenever they allowed him to write. She doesn't want to open them and read them again. The phrases are dry formulas, obvious lies about how well he is and how the jail food is good. He kept sending these letters just to say that he was alive, until the day that there was no letter and she knew that they had put him against the wall.

Underneath the boxes dry petals of jasmine, rose buds, gladiolas and all the flowers of her son's funeral give out a sharp scent. She stares at the boxes, rearranges the contents, and closes their lids and the lid of the big one. She leaves a brief note for her sister next to the prayer bundle and the wooden box, picks up the folded black veil, steps outside, and locks the door.

On the porch, the folded veil over her left arm, she stands facing the late summer evening. The air is light and thin and she breathes it in deeply, keeping it in her lungs as if wanting to hold it there forever. Now she smells the wood smoke of the vendors who grill ears of corn in the nearby market, and she remembers that she has not eaten all day. She decides not to eat tonight and sits on the stone step looking at the darkening flower bed and the orange persimmons hanging like lanterns.

The next-door neighbor, a young woman who likes her, opens her window and calls, "I know you're meditating again, Sima Jaan, but I've cooked some vermicelli soup for my kids. Do you want a bowl?"

"I'm not hungry, dear, thank you. Enjoy it."

"I've left a bowl for you, anyway. Maybe you'll need it tomorrow when your sister comes by."

"Yes, tomorrow, tomorrow—" she says quickly to dismiss her.

The evening gets chilly and she needs to wear something. But she doesn't want to go inside again. The black veil is still hanging on her arm, ceremoniously, like a silk jacket, a piece of formal clothing that might get wrinkled if she lays it down. Should she unfold it and put it on to get warm? She decides not to wear it now. She is not ready yet. She lays the veil on the step next to her and looks at it in the dark. She pats it as if patting the soft back of a house pet and hears something whizzing inside. It's him, she thinks. He's not getting much air in the folds of the veil; he's suffocating.

What else does she need to do? Nothing. What else does she need to say? Nothing.

"I said whatever I needed to say to God, and I'm done. So I better go up on the roof and sleep there tonight. I know it's cold, but I'm not going back into that house again and here the neighbors will see me. The wooden bed is still on the roof. The mosquito net is there too; I'll sleep on the roof tonight."

Excited about sleeping on the roof, she smiles and remembers the many summer nights when the kids were little and the house was warm and they all slept on the roof. The children giggled and played until late and she gazed at the stars, tracing them, naming them. Her husband snored, the children fell asleep, and she lay flat on her back, looking up at the sky. She didn't believe in God then. Not like now. She didn't even think about God. When she was young she didn't wear a veil, either, not even a scarf. She drank beer with her husband many times, and once or twice she had vodka. God came in when they left one by one. No, God came in when she began going to the holy shrines to pray for her son. No. God came earlier, when they arrested her son. Yes, He came to her one night in a dream, as a voice, and said, "You'll need me now. Get up, cover your hair and go to the holy shrine of Ghasem and pray and feed the poor. Go on foot if you want your son to get released." And she did. She woke up early in the morning and packed some bread and cheese and took a thermos of water and wore the black veil, which had been folded for years at the bottom of a trunk. Her daughter asked, Why the veil? She said she was going to wear it from now on. Her daughter asked, Where are you going? She said, To the shrine of Ghasem. Her daughter said, Mother, you don't even remember how to pray. I'll remember soon, she said.

    She walked all day on the edge of a long

road and she found other women, mothers of prisoners, walking to the shrine, and she didn't feel alone. They walked and walked until the sun set and they lodged in a caravansary at night and walked again the next day. Their shoes tore; they bought new ones in remote bazaars and continued walking, until they reached the shrine of the son of the Imam, Ghasem. They prayed in the cool courtyard of the shrine and ate rose water sherbet. They tied a piece of cloth to the post and gave alms to the beggars and walked back. All the while the mothers of the prisoners told stories of their sons and daughters; she listened, but didn't tell any story. What was there to tell? The boy was stubborn, wanted to change the world, and the devil took him. That was all. How could one change the world of God, the world that God had designed?

So these pilgrimages happened three times. Three times God came to her dreams as a deep voice and commanded her to go to a holy shrine and she listened. She went to the shrine of Ghasem, Hassan and Abdullah. She learned chants and prayers she'd never known before. She even went to fortune tellers with the other mothers, and her coffee cup was always as dark as the day of doom.

But all this began with her son's arrest. Before that she drank with her husband, danced at birthday parties, and painted her nails red.

When she was younger her husband paid attention to her nails.
"Don't cut your nails like men. Let them grow. Paint them red! I'll bring some nail polish for you from the store."
She laughed and said, "Then who'll wash the dishes?"
He bought a dishwasher for her, a luxury in those times, just because he loved long red nails. He was an eccentric in some ways; for example, before they went to bed, he liked to watch her changing her clothes. She felt shy and hid behind the closet door, but he craned his neck to see her, or caught her image in the mirror. But in bed he never touched her or even stroked her hair. He just crawled over her like a wet seal, found his way inside her and did his job and crawled back.

Now she caresses the slippery surface of the chador, as if it's a black cat purring next to her. "Be patient, be patient," she whispers. "In a minute."
"So that's when you came," she tells God. "When I went to three shrines on foot with the women and cooked sacred rice pudding and prayed five times a day, you came and stayed and that was when they all left me alone. But didn't I really want them to go? Didn't I feel relieved when they left? I can't lie to you, God. I wanted them to go

and I was relieved when they did."

It began with her husband. The kids were in high school when he died. One day he closed his accessory store and, as usual, bought a watermelon and held it in one arm and carried his business bag in the other hand and walked toward home. The neighbors who saw him that evening say that he collapsed right at the corner of the cul-de-sac where the blind dervish sat with his brass bowl. The watermelon fell and split open. The children who were playing on the sidewalk thought it was the man's brain and blood, and they screamed and ran away. Some men brought him home, but it was too late.

That first night his body was on the bed. The family had to wait until the next day to take him to a morgue. Her son and daughter told her not to sleep in that room, but she didn't listen to them. Poori, who was staying with her, cried and begged her not to go into the bedroom. But when she insisted, they let her alone. They thought it was because of love, grief, and loss. They thought she wanted to lie down next to her husband for the last time. But this was not true. She wanted to undress in the middle of the room, with all the lights on, without him watching her. She wanted to stand there, alone and free, and take all her clothes off with no man peeping or craning his neck to look at her nakedness. She was sad, immensely sad, but so relieved.

Her son gave her trouble. Since the time he began to read in his room all night, since the time he began to go to meetings with his friends and not come home, since the time he began to hide stacks of leaflets under his mattress, he was a trouble. He argued with her and gave her a hard time. He said she didn't understand. There were things she didn't know and would never know, because she was not out in the world. He said the world was rotten and he wanted to change it and make it livable. But he picked the wrong time to change the rotten world, because that was exactly when others were planning to do the same thing in their own ways, and the conflict began.

In his first letter from prison, he wrote, "Mother, don't blame me for your suffering. It's a war, one wins, one loses. We lost."

So she prayed and fasted and walked to the three shrines, and cooked sacred pudding, and gave alms. But nothing worked. The devil pierced the boy with hot bullets against the Wall of The Almighty and since he was an atheist the guards didn't bury him, but brought his corpse home.

Only after digging the flower bed with her daughter and washing him and wrapping him in a white shroud and laying him at the bottom of the cold hole and covering the grave and planting pansies on it, did she feel relief. That night when the smell of freshly dug earth came into the room with the September breeze, she took her tea to the bedroom, opened the window, sat with her tea on the sill, and gave out a long sigh. The boy was dead, lying silently under the earth. No one in this house was going to change the rotten world anymore. She was relieved.

Then she sent her daughter away.

"On purpose, God, on purpose! I sent her away to be alone. I didn't want to hear her crying in her pillow every night. I didn't want her going to typing class hunched under that long, navy uniform. I wanted her to go away and take that scarf off her head and let her hair breathe. But, no, it wasn't just that, it was for me too. I wanted to be by myself."

She murmurs these things, nods sometimes and shakes her head. She pats the black veil once in a while and the scent of camphor rises. She whispers, "In a minute, a minute—"

Night grows deep and dark; silence falls on the neighborhood. Now it's time for her to go up to the roof and sleep. What if she leaves the veil here? What if she tricks the small, narrow thing that is now hissing in a dark corner? But it's cold up there, she doesn't have a jacket with her and she is not going back inside that house again. She needs the chador to keep her warm.

On the roof, she sits on the damp, wooden cot that has been there since old times, when they didn't have the air conditioner and they slept on the roof. The bed is dusty and smells of mildew. She sits on the edge and puts the folded chador next to her. She imagines unfolding the veil, then lying down and covering her body, now closing her eyes and letting the small creature do whatever he has come to do.

Will her sister check the roof tomorrow? Will anyone check the rooftop?

She sits on the edge of the bed, looks up at the stars, the familiar stars of her past, the ones she traced and counted many times. She shivers. The September breeze becomes cool and strong, turns into a wind, and she feels that she needs to wrap something around her shoulders. She looks at the veil, sitting there in its heavy folds, heaving and throbbing, pulsating like a living thing. She picks it up, gently, and walks to the edge of the roof. She stands there looking down at the square courtyard and the round pool in the middle, the persimmon tree, the lanterns of the ripening fruits, and the pansies sleeping shyly in the dark. She takes a deep breath and thinks about tomorrow,

Friday, when Poori will show up at ten o'clock to spend the day with her. They'll sew some, then they'll cook for the week; they'll eat together in front of the television, and take a nap on the porch. They may go out to the market and shop, or they may plant new flowers in the flower bed. Poori will stay until evening when her husband will come to pick her up. They'll chat all day while doing these things, they'll reminisce, they'll laugh. They'll eat the neighbor's vermicelli soup too, which always tastes better after it has sat overnight. The day will pass quickly and the new week will begin—the yard, the chores, the prayers and the folding and unfolding of many scented cloths—the chador, the cashmere, the kerchief—and telling and retelling her stories to God.

Reviewing all this in her mind she smiles and feels something lapping inside her, something like a small tide—lapping and lapping, repeating a rhythm that extends to the coming autumn, the winter, and the next spring, to many seasons, as long as she wishes. She feels a vague joy, imagining a snowy day, when suddenly the sun comes out and the world glows like an immense diamond. New tides lap in her and make her giggle. Now, slowly, she shakes the black veil and spreads it open. The wind blows from the west and she holds the veil up in the air, letting it wave and quiver like a gigantic flag. She laughs louder now and says, "I tricked you, little devil, I rinsed my chador with the wind!"

She is standing at the edge of the roof now, Sima, a woman of fifty, holding the very end of a wide chador, making it dance in waves. Now, in an instant, she feels that she doesn't need this piece of cloth anymore. What if she let it go? She opens her fingers and lets the veil fly into the night sky, like a bat, or an ominous bird. She watches it floating and flapping its wings, and she wonders where it will land, or if it will land at all. Wind dishevels her graying hair; she shivers with pleasure and lets the breeze play in the strands of her hair.

THE POOL

A few days after all the thick-braided girls became bald they took us to the courtyard. The empty pool lay dry and dusty under the sun. I'd once seen them whipping the girls here. They told us to stand around the pool. The August day was hot; even this early, sweat bubbled on my face and wet my armpits. Now I noticed that the ground was covered with pebbles. I remembered that the courtyard had a red brick floor. Obviously they had brought pebbles overnight and covered the brick. No one knew what was going on. Armed Revolutionary Guards stood around, aiming their machine guns at us.

Then they brought more inmates out—all women—from the temporary and the permanent cells. They brought the atheists, the infidels, the Baha'is, the monarchists, and those who were ideologically unidentified. We were the first group, so they prodded us closer to the edge of the pool. Now the pockmarked woman, the woman with long, dagger- shaped eyebrows whose name always slipped my mind, dragged a girl by a leash and pushed her into the empty pool. An armed female guard dragged another girl and did the same thing to her. They dumped the girls like garbage bags into the dusty pool. Hadj-Jamali, the jailer and a Devotee of the Holy Revolution, appeared from one of the chambers around the pool. He looked sleepy. One button on his big belly had popped open. The sun was in his eyes. He held his right hand over his eyebrows. He was irritated. He raised his voice.

"We're going to stone these whores today. If you don't cooperate, you'll end up down there yourselves. Understood?"

"But why?" someone, a tiny voice from my left side, asked.

"Who said 'why'? There must be a reason. We're not crazy or idle, to spend our time stoning people. It shames me to tell you why. I can't talk about it. Sister, can you find the right words to explain this punishment?" he asked the pockmarked woman.

"I'll try, Brother Jamali," she said in her husky voice. "These dirty bitches are sick. Perverted. You know what I mean? The repentant sister who sleeps in their cell woke up last night to have a sip of water and she saw them in each other's arms. You get me?"

"Enough now!" Hadj-Jamali said. "Now they know." He looked impatient. He wanted to get this over with and go to his cool office. "Pick a stone and teach them a lesson. If you don't cooperate, it means you approve of their act."

Jamali, the pockmarked woman, the armed female guards, and some veiled repentants whose number had increased each lifted a stone and threw it at the girls in the pool. The inmates were hesitant. Some girls cried.

"Do you want to go down in the pool? Huh? Pick up a stone. This is an order!"

Some girls picked up a very small pebble and threw it. The first ones were slow and careful, then the rhythm became faster. There was a shower of stones on the girls in the pool. They were on all fours like animals, protecting themselves with their arms curved around their heads. All of a sudden a sharp thing jabbed me in my belly; it was the barrel of a gun.

"Pick up a stone, bitch! Hurry up, or you'll go down too." This was a hooded repentant. I'd heard trustworthy repentants could carry guns.

I picked up a pebble and threw it in the pool. Then I picked up others. None hit them. I kept doing this so the repentant would leave me alone. Many girls didn't cooperate. The guards pushed them into the pool and the others hit them.

Now there were several women in the pool and I could see the blood. I tried not to look at the pool, at the bloody heads and the bruised bodies.

But it was hard not to look. How long was this to go on? Why wouldn't they stop? They kept throwing and I saw more blood and more girls being prodded into the pool. I threw and threw, not controlling my aim anymore, not being careful not to hurt anyone. I threw the stones because this hooded repentant who looked like a raven pressed the barrel of her gun to my belly, and if I'd stopped picking up stones and throwing them at the girls, she'd either push me into the bloody pool or shoot me. I threw more, not looking to see if the stones were big or small, round or sharp. So I hit my cellmates until someone next to me screamed with horror. She was Roya, the highschool girl they'd arrested a week ago for possessing flyers. The scream came from the bottom of her lungs and pierced my eardrums. She shrieked, ripped her scarf, and bared her bald head. Her skull looked strangely yellow and small, like an unripe cantaloupe. She tore her black uniform open, undressed, shrieked again, and jumped in the pool of dust and blood.

In the chaos of dust, screams, and gunshots, I called Roya, but she couldn't hear me. I'm not sure why I kept calling her. Almost all of us were screaming now. Roya was rolling among the bloody women, now embracing them, now kissing them, even licking their bloody heads. She was crying, crying for them and with them, until they fired so many bullets into the air that the whole world became quiet.

Then there was such a silence that I heard a mockingbird singing somewhere in a tree outside the prison. The bird was trying to imitate human sound.

They took us back to the cell and turned the radio up loud so that we'd have to listen to the sermons of the Ayatollahs who advised us to repent and return to the bosom of Allah. Soon they fed us rice and eggplant stew with big chunks of meat swimming in the red juice. The commotion was over and we were calm.

This happened a while ago. After the stoning, nothing was intolerable or even very painful for me, neither the sound of bullets in the heart of the night, nor the sermons bouncing off the cell's brick walls. I was calm and content and nothing could make me cry. I never asked my cellmates if they felt the same as I did.

THE DARK END OF THE ORCHARD

Among all the relatives, friends, colleagues, and acquaintances that we lost in one way or another in the 1979 Revolution or as a result of it, Uncle Halali's loss is the strangest of all. He was my grandfather's stepbrother and lived on the skirt of Mount Alborz in a neighborhood north of the Zargande River. He was a math teacher, taught at Riverbank's Boys' Elementary, and his wife Behi was the neighborhood seamstress. She mostly did alteration jobs and once in a while made a dress for an affluent lady. The Halalis had four children that had all turned bad like the rotten apples in their orchard. The children had left home early, and Uncle Halali and Behi lived together in their two-room clay hut at the end of the apple orchard.

It may sound unusual, but Uncle Halali's house was not a house in the real sense of the word; it was an apple orchard that didn't bear good apples. Every autumn crooked, ugly apples full of worms, not even good for jam or pickles, covered the ground, and the poor old couple had to work day and night to sack them and throw them away. Uncle Halali had inherited this orchard from his father and was stuck with it. The orchard was a burden hanging on his neck. Of the two rooms at the end of the orchard, which Uncle built when he married Behi, one served as kitchen, the other as bedroom and living room. They slept in this room every night and piled the mattresses and quilts in a corner every morning to open a space for the folding table and four folding chairs. No one knows how they managed to live in these two rooms when all their children were still around.

As long as I can remember, Uncle Halali was an old man. When I was a child and went to Riverbank's Girls' Elementary, next to the boys' school, I saw Uncle walking along the river, watching his feet. Then I saw him take the same path back to his orchard at the end of a cul-de-sac. I always waved to him, but he never raised his head to see people, or the trees, or the sky.

Uncle Halali was tall and skeletal, his hair thin and gray. He wore thick, round lenses, so thick they looked like the bottom of drinking glasses. Although he wasn't lame, he used a cane. Some say he used a cane because his eyes were weak. You see, three times in his life, Uncle Halali fell into the river, right at the same spot where an ancient pomegranate tree, barren for a long time, stands alone gathering dust. Uncle's eyes were so bad that he did not see the edge of the pathway as he neared it, the huge tree concealed the river, and he slipped down into the shallow water, falling onto the sharp rocks. Once the baker and twice passers-by saved him. Fortunately the Zargande River never had much water. Uncle just got some bruises, lost his cane once, and broke his eyeglasses twice.

As to what went on in his head, what preoccupied him such that he fell in the river or lost his way in the narrow alleys, no one knew. But after the second fall, Aunty Behi put all of his books in sacks and returned them to Grandfather.

"Halali reads too much, Abbas Khan! Please don't bring him books anymore. If he falls in the damn river one more time, he won't survive."

But, as I said before, he fell one more time, and sooner than you'd imagine, his bookshelf was full of thick books again.

Uncle Halali was a quiet man. I can't remember his voice; I can't remember him talking. Once in a while Grandfather took me to his place, more to check on his stepbrother than to visit him. These rituals were boring for me, but I went with Grandfather so as not to hurt his feelings. We sat around the folding table, Aunty Behi served us some tea and sugar cubes (she never had fruit, nuts, or pastries to offer), and Grandfather, who was a good speaker, lectured about something, enjoying his own eloquence. I remember that most of the time the subject Grandfather raised was the comparison between classical poetry and free verse, which he fervently condemned as artless and meaningless. Uncle Halali sipped his tea and listened, his head slightly bent. He never expressed his opinion.

Once when I asked my mother why Grandfather had a big house and Uncle Halali lived in a clay room she drew a complicated family tree for me. I didn't make much sense out of it and now all I can remember is that Grandfather's father was a Cossack who emigrated from Russia to Iran with his wife and children—three daughters and a son. The Cossack went into the horse-breeding business and in a short time became wealthy. His wife, my grandfather's mother, died and the Cossack married another woman. This woman, who was just divorced from an abusive husband, brought her little son to the Cossack's house. Grandfather, who was fifteen years old and the only son of his father, suddenly found himself with a little brother, a four-year-old, for whom he soon became responsible. They were not from the same blood, but they grew up as brothers, or rather as a young father and a son. Grandfather's father, the Cossack horse breeder, died, and for some reason that I didn't quite understand, or for the simple reason that Ahmad Halali was not his real son, he didn't include him in his will. Halali was a young, penniless man when he left the Cossack's house to find his own fortune. His fortune turned out to be a girl by the name of Behi with whom he fell in love. Meanwhile Ahmad Halali's real father died and left him an apple orchard but nothing else.

  The stepbrothers lived different lives. Grandfather sold his father's horse-breeding business and, because of his love of literature, opened a publishing and book-binding company. Uncle Halali went to a teacher-training school and became a math teacher. Although the stepbrothers belonged to different classes now, they still shared certain things, books being the most important of them. Grandfather, who used to take care of this man when he was a little boy, continued to visit him and check on him, but he never gave him money to improve his life or to add a toilet to the two rooms so that the couple didn't have to use the outhouse on cold winter nights.

  When I asked my mother why Grandfather didn't help Uncle Halali, she just sighed and said, "Even real brothers don't help each other, what do you expect from a stepbrother? Look at your Uncle Rahman who lives in a mansion and has a villa at the Caspian Sea. And look at us. How long is it that I've been dreaming about changing this dirty wallpaper and I can't? Does your Uncle Rahman help your father? And they're blood brothers, too. Haven't you heard the saying, 'We may be brothers, but our accounts are different'?"

The most curious thing about this old, silent uncle of ours was his love for his wife. The couple had a reputation for this. It was no secret that Ahmad Halali and Behi Halali were old lovers. While most people's marriages were only a contract for the wife to do the household chores and produce babies and the husband to earn the money, Uncle Halali and Behi lived differently. Behi tended to the house and the orchard and earned half of their income by her needlework, Uncle made the other half by his meager teacher's salary and helped his wife at home. They divided the work equally.

But this wasn't the whole story. Everybody knew that Aunty Behi had a nasty case of arthritis. Her knuckles were getting larger and larger every day and she couldn't walk properly. Her legs were bowed like two parentheses, her knee joints protruded in a strange way. There were rumors that every night Uncle Halali massaged Behi's enlarged joints with some homemade ointment, a combination of coconut oil and seven mountain herbs. He rubbed his wife's joints one by one—toes, fingers, knees, and crooked spine, vertebra by vertebra. How this private ritual had become common knowledge, only God knows. But there was more evidence of the couple's love than the massage. I was a child and didn't notice these things, but they say when Uncle Halali sat in his folding chair to grade his students' homework, Behi hovered around his chair like a half-burned moth around a candle, serving him food, covering his shoulders with a blanket, rubbing his tired neck, and whatnot.

Why the four children of such a peaceful couple should turn bad, no one knows. As no one can ever figure out why among all the orchards of the Riverbank area, Halali's orchard should be rotten. My mother always said that Uncle Halali and his wife Behi gave so much love to each other that nothing was left for the kids; the children were neglected. But I never believed that. Grandfather sighed and said that Ahmad's star from the beginning was a bad star and he recited a line of classical poetry about people who are born with bad stars. "Who knoweth the decree writ for him by destiny?"

The Halalis' first child, at the age of nineteen, robbed a local bank and went to prison for ten years. When he was released he disappeared from the face of the earth. They say he was involved in more serious crimes, collaborating with a famous gang he joined in prison. The second son went into military service, got stationed in a remote village on the border, made a village girl pregnant, and was forced to marry her and stay there. No one ever learned his whereabouts. Some said he had seven children by the village girl and worked in the rice fields; others believed he had run away, crossed the border and got himself lost in foreign lands. Halali's third child was a girl; she eloped with the neighbor's boy when she was fifteen, lost her virginity, the boy left her and she never returned home. She lived with certain women in the "New City," a neighborhood respectable people would never go to.

The fourth child, another girl, was crazy. She began showing symptoms when she was thirteen. She went to the dark end of the orchard every night and talked to invisible people. She ate mud and smeared it on her naked body. She danced weird dances and made obscene gestures. The poor couple tried to keep her in the house, but when she began to cut herself with razor blades and suck her own blood, they took her to the crazy house and that's where she stayed for the rest of her life. The couple visited her once in a while, took fresh clothes and food for her, but when she didn't recognize them anymore they stopped going.

In their last years, Uncle Halali and his wife looked even older than they'd always looked. Uncle's back was stooped and his eyes were almost blind. Behi's knuckles were each the size of a large walnut, her knees almost as big as honeydew melons. She walked on all fours. At night, neighbors could hear Behi moaning with pain and pleasure when her old husband rubbed her big joints with the ointment. They say she looked like a large tarantula when she crawled. The four kids, the bad apples, were forgotten, and in the whole universe there were just the two of them—the old man and the old lady. Uncle retired from teaching and the couple spent long days and nights together in the two clay rooms at the end of the orchard.

Everybody knows that winter nights are tough in the foothills, especially at the bank of the Zargande River. Wolves howl on the hills, stray dogs bark all night, and snow falls not in flakes, but in large, thick patches. On such nights one can imagine a small kerosene heater burning in the Halalis' living room, the husband and wife sitting together, feeling warm and safe with their loaf of bread and a pot of hot tea. Not much to look forward to. No grandchildren to babysit. No money to plan a summer vacation. No sweet memories they can recall. All bad memories they'd rather forget. So the present is all there is. The bread, the tea, enough kerosene in the heater, and the constant whiz of the water boiling on top of the fire. They don't talk, just sit, Aunty bent over a stitching job, Uncle reading an old book that has extra large letters and is the only book he can read now.

When I say everything about Uncle Halali's life and death was curious I have strong reasons for it. Just imagine how he should die—not in the peace and quiet of his winter night, bending over his book; not lying down next to the warm body of his beloved Behi; not in his familiar river either, lying flat on the sharp stones; but at a brick wall. They say that the guards made him stand at the Wall of the Almighty with twelve other prisoners all much younger than him, all political. They were machine-gunned. What was Uncle Halali doing there? No one can figure this out.

In those years I wasn't around anymore, so what I'm saying is what I hear from family and friends. They say that on one of those rainy winter nights the black prison van stopped at the end of the dark cul-de-sac where Uncle Halali's orchard was. Five tall, bearded guards invaded the two small rooms; they handcuffed, blindfolded, and prodded Uncle Halali into the van. He was in his blue pajamas. They didn't let him wear his robe. They say Aunty Behi was so shocked that she neither talked nor screamed for help. She stood there motionless, her jaws locked, watching the bearded guards take her old husband away. Only when they left did she pick up her husband's eyeglasses and limp toward the door.

Uncle's imprisonment was brief, not more than a week. Eight days after the arrest, the same van brought his corpse home. They wouldn't bury the communists and infidels in the cemeteries; they either dumped them in a common grave or returned the corpses to their families to bury them in their own houses. The common grave was already full, so they brought Uncle home.

People who tell me the story of Uncle Halali's burial may exaggerate the scene, but even when I try to reduce the dramatic tension, it still breaks my heart. They say it was raining for seven days and nights, the dirt was black mud that froze at night. The cold mountain wind lashed people like a whip. Barefoot and bareheaded, Behi swayed on her bowed legs and carried a shovel from the house. She dug a grave at the end of the orchard by herself. If a neighbor approached to offer help, she screamed and chased him away. She dug the grave in the frozen mud. She limped back to the house, washed and groomed her husband, sprayed rose water on him, and wrapped him in one of the sheets they used to sleep under. As to how she carried the heavy corpse to the grave, my imagination doesn't help me much. Maybe she had acquired supernatural powers. This can happen to people sometimes. She lay the corpse in the grave and, not with the shovel but with her hands, filled the hole. She covered the surface of the grave with dead leaves and rotten apples.

This was the beginning of winter. Soon the rain turned to snow and the snow covered Uncle Halali's grave and all the leaves and apples that sat on top of it.

Aunty Behi lived for only two months after she buried her husband. The neighbors could hear her moaning, almost howling, every night like one of those she-wolves that lived in the hills. Some believe that she mourned for Halali and released all the sounds she couldn't let out the night they took her husband away, but others say she cried from pain, physical pain, pain of the large joints, because there was no one to rub them with coconut ointment every night.

As to why Uncle Halali was arrested and executed at age sixty-five, there is more than one story. Some say it was all because of that book he kept reading every night. It was the *Communist Manifesto* in large print. As a person who contemplated everything and wanted to learn what he didn't know, Halali studied Marxism to make sense of the student movements, the uprisings and the street fights. Someone must have reported him. Others believe that Halali had converted to the Baha'i religion after his retirement and the book he was reading was the prayer book of the Baha'is. He was executed as an infidel.

There is a third group who says that the book was a collection of ghazals his stepbrother had printed for him in large letters. But there are also a few who believe that the book was not an issue at all and the whole thing was a mistake, a misunderstanding. The guards took Halali for someone else, one of the communist leaders who was hiding in the Zargande area in a friend's orchard.

There is no way to know now. Aunty Behi is dead. She was buried by the neighbors next to Uncle Halali in the apple orchard. The clay rooms and the outhouse have been leveled and the few items of furniture and that mysterious book with large letters boxed and thrown away. No one was there to claim them. All the four possibilities are equally believable: Learning Marxism to make sense of the revolution? Reading poetry in his leisure? Converting to another religion in his old age? Or just his bad star rising high again? I'm sure Grandfather would pick this last option if he were alive. He would say, "Look! Among all the old men wearing thick lenses, living at the end of cul-de-sacs, Ahmad Halali must be mistaken for a political leader. 'Who knoweth the decree writ for him by destiny?'"

But what strikes me as the saddest of all is the fact that life is going on in the Riverbank neighborhood as if nothing had happened. The baker who has been baking for half a century on the east bank of the river still bakes, the Riverbank's Boys' Elementary is open and every year a new generation of little boys sits in the same old wooden chairs and grabs their half-eaten pencils with their dirty wind-burnt hands, and the new math teacher, smeared with white chalk from head to foot, writes on the same cracked blackboard that Uncle Halali used to write on. The orchard, now the government's property, is there, bearing the same rotten apples fall after fall. And life goes on. All that is missing are the two small rooms that contained Ahmad Halali and his wife Behi for forty-five years. The old, silent couple vanished as if they had never existed, and people forgot them even before that long winter was over.

THE STORY OF OUR LIFE

I'm happy that you finally found me. The last time you wrote (fifteen or sixteen years ago?) you were publishing a weekly newspaper. You enclosed an issue. It looked promising. Although you'd used a pseudonym, I recognized your prose. I wrote you back. But you didn't write and didn't send the paper again. I didn't write either. Then at some point I lost your address and I thought I'd lost you forever. Now you're saying that all these years you have been sending me your newspaper. Dear friend, are you sure you have been sending them to me? Have you confused me with someone else? You might have sent them to the wrong address. I haven't moved. At least I'm sure about this! In any case, when I didn't receive anything from you, I thought that your paper had failed and you had lost hope. I thought you had plunged into depression. Inactivity. You had cut yourself off from your friends. Now I'm happy to know that you've been publishing your paper for the past fifteen or sixteen years.

In your kind letter, which has a vague touch of nostalgia, you regret my wasted talent. "You could have become a great writer," you write.

"What happened? Why did you stop writing?"

I never stopped writing, my dear. I'm still writing and will write to the end. But for a complicated reason which I will try to explain, I can never reach the final draft of my manuscript. But it doesn't matter anymore. I call it "my manuscript" because some time after we last met (almost twenty years ago in Dustland), I stopped writing those bits and pieces that I used to write and started a long piece. This long piece was supposed to be about the life that we all lived back home, before our exile. My initial plan was to write about that life—which you yourself are aware of—the strange diversity of its incidents and the peculiar intensity of its outcomes. I wanted to write it on several levels:

1. To use the materials of real life, i.e., what really happened to us.

2. To use the materials of my dreams, which all, in one way or another, were related to those incidents. I had collected them in several notebooks.

3. To write about what could have happened instead of what did happen, and the dreams I could have had and never had.

So I started. But here I have to pause and tell you that I stopped writing in our native language. Lack of contact with our land, the people and the language itself made it impossible for me to continue thinking and writing in our language. It was dead for me. So it took me a good while to master the language of the country I was residing in.

When I received your last letter, fifteen or sixteen years ago, with one issue of your newspaper and the promise of more to come, I was playing with the idea of the long piece. I started it shortly after that—about fifteen years ago.

The way I wrote this piece (and I'm still writing it!) may surprise you. It surprises me. I wrote chapter after chapter without having time to go back and revise. Every morning I woke up with new images, characters, and incidents in my head. I sat and worked. For money, I took an evening job. My older characters would grow old and die and new ones would live and dream. The old ones would appear in the dreams of the young ones and would live yet another life. The incidents, as I said before, at first were the stuff of real life, what happened to us back home and in Dustland. But later, these incidents showed themselves in different forms. To make a long story short, dear friend, I wrote ninety-two chapters—almost 2,000 pages. This is longer than any existing novel. But I told our story.

For eleven years, I wrote every single day

and didn't have time to go back and read what I had written. But do you think when I finally wrote the last line and put in the final period I felt happy? Content? Relieved? Not a bit.

Now I had to read it. As you can guess, it took me a long time to read the manuscript and make notes for revision. Major revisions were needed. Mountainous. Not to speak of the problems with the language, my use of which was quite raw when I started but matured as I progressed. There were characters who appeared in the first chapters but whom I had forgotten and abandoned midway. There were incidents which didn't serve any purpose and should have been omitted, but their absence would damage certain other incidents which were quite necessary for the story.

After reading each chapter, I wept.

The process of revision started. I had no time to waste. I was growing old. Soon it became enjoyable. It took me years.

Meanwhile, some friends (I still had some people around me and had not become isolated) suggested that I should send some pieces, or as they put it, "chunks," out and try to get them published. The way I was working, they believed, I deserved recognition and encouragement. I tried that. But it was very time consuming. To prepare a piece meant to revise it, edit it, type it, proofread it, make it presentable, and send it out. This took all my morning hours—my only writing time. And what did I gain? The publishers wrote back—those who responded—that the piece was ambiguous. Complicated. What went before? What after? Send us a synopsis. It took me three months to prepare a synopsis. When I attached the synopsis to the piece, the publishers stopped responding all together. They must have considered me a lunatic. The synopsis was overwhelming. They couldn't believe such a life had been lived.

I decided not to waste my precious time anymore. I went back to my everyday routine of writing and revising. I did some public readings too. The same friends arranged readings for me. Ten or fifteen people showed up, listened politely, and left in confusion. You know, it's impossible to get anything out of this story by listening to just a few pages. The whole thing must be read from beginning to end.

So as not to feel lonely, I took it to writing workshops. The bits and pieces I read in the workshops were murdered on the spot. I locked myself in.

I'm working on the third draft now. It needs work. Human life is short. What if I've reached the last stop?

I've aged. Everything around me has changed. My children have grown up and left. I lost their childhood. They have their own children now. The old man died three years ago. The few months in and out of the hospital were the only time I didn't write on schedule. I'd sneak out of bed, wrap a blanket around myself and go up to the cold study and work every night till morning. Those few months of working at night damaged the manuscript. Later I had to change all those parts. I'm a different person at night, my characters behave differently.

I said that I've become old. I realized this today when I was trying to tie the garbage bag and put a fresh one in the can. It was an effort. Almost impossible. I left the bag open, spilling out. But writing is not an effort. Has never been an effort.

When I revise, I make major changes. It is, in fact, like creating the piece again. I add new characters; they create new situations with new consequences. These situations and consequences affect the general plot, and the old situations and consequences are not needed anymore. A new thing is being born out of the old all the time. The red bird emerges out of its own ashes, so to speak. I murder a major character who has survived two revisions and add a new one. The dreams we all dream, my characters and I, have no limit. What

we imagine has no boundaries. There is no horizon in this universe.
     So it's not that I'm not writing! You haven't read anything of me and most probably you never will. I'm writing in a language you do not know, but about a life you've lived. You can remember that life better than I can. You and all my other friends who never attempted to tell the story of our life can remember it more clearly than I, who spent my life narrating it. In the long process of telling the story, I thought about it, imagined it, dreamed it, and wrote it in so many forms, so many times, that the story changed into something else and I lost the real one altogether. I have created a new story which is not the story of our life and will not stay the way it is.
     I'm writing all this responding to your friendly but regretful remark about my lost talent as a writer.
     My dear, I'd like to end this letter with my last image of you. You may or may not remember that the last time we met we were in your apartment in the country that, for security reasons, we all called Dustland. It was a farewell scene. You had leaned back against the wall. One knee bent, foot on the wall. Your hands in your pockets. You were pale, avoiding my eyes. Your little boys were kissing my little girls. Your beautiful wife

was shaking hands with my husband. You and I embraced briefly. We left. I didn't hear from you until a few years later when I was residing in the second country after our exile. I was still writing bits and pieces in our native language, although the language was slipping away from me. I received another letter from you in the third country of my residence (here). This is the letter in which you informed me that you had moved out of Dustland and were publishing a newspaper. You included one issue which was quite fine and you promised to send it to me regularly.

    Dear friend, all these years you've either confused me with someone else and have sent your papers to her, or you have used a wrong address. As I mentioned before, I haven't moved. But there is another possibility: how can I be sure that you have really continued publishing your paper and you are not living in delusion, as most of our friends are?

    In any case, if your handsome boys are still around, kiss them for me. They must be gentlemen now, married and all. And send my regards to your wife. Write to me. I have more time now. I've retired from my evening job and, as I said, I never write at night.

P.S. Send me your newspapers and a family pic-

ture.
P.P.S. Were we in love? If we were, was it back home, or in Dustland? Did we sleep in each other's arms one cold winter night? This is the way I vaguely picture the scene:
It was snowing outside. You were at our place. It was curfew and you couldn't go home. My husband was stuck somewhere; he couldn't get home. My daughters were asleep. You were anxious. You called your wife and said that you couldn't leave our place because of the curfew. There was nothing to be done. The night was long. We opened a bottle of vodka and drank it together. We didn't talk much, just listened to the tanks moving toward the mountain where the war was. Then we kissed. Maybe we were afraid. I don't remember our emotions anymore. We almost undressed, but then we fell asleep without making love. In our sleep we could hear random gunshots, explosions, the rattling of machine guns and the roar of the tanks. You slipped out before dawn.
Did this happen, or is it what I've written somewhere in one of the many drafts of my story? Now I wonder if I have kept this episode. It's worth keeping. What if I've crossed it out? You don't need to try to remember. It's an awfully long time ago. Just write to me. It's good that you've finally found me.

THE UNBELIEVABLE STORY OF MY GRANDFATHER'S WIFE

Who knows who Tuba was or where she came from? She appeared as if with a gust, lived with Grandfather for thirteen years, then disappeared like a shadow from the wall.

The way I remember her is so different from the way my brother does that sometimes I think we're not talking about the same Tuba. What I remember is a small woman with large breasts and rounded hips, hair henna-red, curly, and down to her shoulders, but puffed up like a lion's mane. Tuba always wore heavy make-up—blue and green eye shadow and blood-red lipstick which left marks on people's cheeks when she kissed them. I was ten when she appeared in our lives. I adored her. She was the most beautiful when she danced.

My brother, who was five years old when we first saw Tuba, remembers our stepgrandmother as a horrible woman, scary and grotesque.

"Tuba looked like a witch," he says. "Her wild red hair and long red nails frightened me. When she laughed, I wanted to scream."

"Do you remember the jingle of her coins?"

"What coins?"

My brother doesn't remember the purse of coins in Tuba's throat. If he did, he'd accuse her of being a real witch.

When we first saw Tuba, Grandfather must have been a handsome middle-aged man. He brought his girlfriend to the New Year's party to introduce her to the family. This was the big annual family gathering, and I'm sure Grandfather knew how he was going to shock everyone. He always enjoyed offending his family, especially his mother, by injuring their sense of moral righteousness.

My mother remembers that that night all the women had gathered around Grand-Lady's special recliner, breaking and spitting sunflower hulls like a gang of hungry parrots, talking about Tuba until midnight. No one could guess who this woman was and why she looked and acted the way she did.

In those days in traditional Iranian families women wouldn't smoke or drink or dance or even laugh aloud. All through the night Tuba drank vodka with the men, told dirty jokes, and laughed wildly and loudly. When she became warm enough, she kicked off her velvet pumps and threw her big shawl, with the picture of a strange peacock printed on it, on Grandfather's lap, leaping to the center of the room. I remember Tuba's dance more than anything else, it tickled my insides, made me feel like thrusting my arms apart and stamping my feet to death. Tuba whirled and wriggled, shook different parts of her body, and made an enormous umbrella with her rainbowed skirt. Men held their breath and hid their erections; women bit their lips and pinched their cheeks hard. When she finished dancing, I gathered her pumps and held them in my arms for a while. These small shoes, almost my size, looked magical to me. They were made of black velvet and many starry sequins glittered on them.

Gasping and laughing with joy, Tuba lifted her thick hair up with her right hand to fan her hot neck with the left. Her bare armpits showed as her red silk sleeves slipped over her shoulders. Unseen and unheard of—who was she and where had she come from? She couldn't be a Moslem woman, she must be either a Jew or a Gypsy—a Gypsy-Jew, maybe. The women hulled tons of sunflower seeds and talked behind Tuba's back. They talked and talked, but didn't get anywhere.

Grandfather married Tuba shortly after that New Year's party and Grand-Lady, his mother, stopped talking to him. His sisters, my great aunts, stopped talking to him, and his daughters, my aunts, and his daughters-in-law, my uncles' wives, stopped talking to him. But men stayed friendly with Grandfather, teasing him about his choice of a wife. They were jealous of him, of course. His sons were the most jealous. "Father has gone mad," they said.

Tuba was fond of my brother who was the prettiest child in the whole family. She took him on her lap, caressing his long curls, whispering things into his ears. I remember my brother staring at her painted face, playing with the big loops of her gold earrings. But now he doesn't remember all this and keeps repeating that Tuba was a witch.

"She was a real witch," he says. "That's why she appeared and disappeared the way she did. That's why she came to Grandfather's funeral in a black veil and disappeared when we chased her into the alley."

After Tuba took my brother on her lap, kissing him and stroking his curls, she hit the glands between her round chin and her small ear, making a sound as if a purse of coins rattled in her throat. I curled beside Tuba, watching her and smelling her. She smelled of rose water and something that only later I discovered was called camphor, then used in mortuaries to disinfect corpses. I sat there next to Tuba, but she never talked to me or even looked at me.

In those years I was a dark little girl with short thin hair (so thin that my white scalp showed) and a nose a bit big for my mousy face. My eyes were weak and I had to wear a pair of black-rimmed eye-glasses, rectangular in shape, made for men. When I went to school a bunch of street urchins followed me, chanting a song they'd made for me: "Froggy, froggy goes to school, wearing glasses like a fool—"

I wasn't just plain and unattractive; I was ugly. That's why I would make myself invisible when I wished. Especially at parties and big family gatherings, I sat in a corner forever without being noticed. If I didn't approach the table, timidly, to take some food, no one would invite me to eat. My parents often forgot about me unless they needed me to baby-sit the younger children. I don't think Tuba even saw me when I sat next to her, watching her neck, listening to the rattle of her purse.

But the women of the family didn't despise Tuba for long. Tuba's fortune-telling skills attracted them to her. Like crazy moths dancing around a burning candle, women gathered around Tuba, listening to her predictions. Tuba's voice was different from other women's voices. It was deep and husky, even a bit scratchy. This could have been because of all the cigarettes she smoked. When Tuba bent over a coffee cup, she squinted, sighed, and whispered to her customer, "I can see a thick black lump sitting on your heart. But a light is shining through this mirror. Look! See for yourself!" And she held the cup under her client's bewildered eyes.

Both my brother and I remember Tuba's small fortune-telling room, with a strange beaded curtain hanging in the doorway instead of a door. In the middle of the room there was a small table surrounded by four chairs. A pot of blood-red geraniums graced the table. We went there so many times with our mother and aunts and sat there and listened to Tuba telling their fortunes that the smell of fresh Turkish coffee, the old deck of Tarot cards, and the bitter scent of geraniums are still in our nostrils. So when the women realized that Tuba could predict certain things about their future they stopped criticizing her. They especially respected her when she predicted my cousin's release from prison.

My older aunt, Effat, had a son in the Castle, the central prison during the Shah's regime. His name was Naser; he was a political prisoner on death row. His parents had sent him to Europe to become an engineer, but instead he went to and then returned from China with a group of his friends to topple the monarchy and start a peasant's revolution in the Chinese style. He was arrested the very first week and locked up in Unit Four, the maximum security unit of the Castle. No one talked about the incident, because Aunty Effat would have serious fits, but everyone knew that they tortured Naser in the Castle's dark chambers.

Tuba looked into Aunty Effat's dark coffee cup, narrowed her painted eyes, and said, "I don't see death here! I see a mirror and lots of flowers and candles in it. This looks more like a wedding to me than an execution!"

The next week, cousin Naser sent a letter from the Castle that he had decided to sign the necessary papers (meaning cooperating with the secret police). He couldn't write that the torture was intolerable; he wrote that he missed his mother and that he would be out soon.

When Naser was released, my aunt's family carried tons of flowers and pastries, candles and mirrors to the gate of the Castle and escorted their son to Tuba's house. They threw coins at Tuba's feet and crowned her with flowers. But this was not Tuba's last fortune-telling. Among many minor prophecies—kids passing their exams, young girls getting married, husbands and wives making up again, and so on—I remember the time when she saw Grand-Lady's eventual recovery in Grandfather's coffee cup. Grand-Lady, who was suffering from a fatal kidney disease, recovered miraculously and all the tubes and machines that had been attached to her since she had come back from the hospital were disconnected. Soon she began walking and bossing everybody around. Again, Tuba was crowned by flowers and rewarded with large, heavy, gold coins.

"Here is all my gold," Tuba tilted her head, hitting her glands with the tip of her fingers. Her throat rattled like a purse full of coins. "Do you want to feel my purse?" she asked my brother, but he said no and shied away. I slipped onto the couch and sat very close to Tuba, touching the corner of the silk scarf loosely covering her shoulder, but she didn't notice me.

Grandfather and Tuba were in love. They lived in a small cage of an apartment in a busy downtown neighborhood, spending all day together, eating and drinking, listening to music and making love. Grandfather had retired from his tedious job as an accountant in the Ministry of Planning and Budgeting, but he was growing younger instead of older. Everybody knew how the couple partied together, drank vodka and ate Tuba's special cutlets. They stayed up every night and slept all morning.

Women sat around Grand-Lady's recliner, gossiping about Tuba. Since she was their fortune teller now, and they needed her, their gossip was either good gossip or had a double meaning. Double-meaning gossip was sarcastic, seemingly told with good intentions, but really with a mean spirit. For example my younger aunt, Monir, who had a terrible marriage (her husband had a mistress), would say, "Look! This is the way to keep a husband. We all have to learn from Tuba. Do you see the way she takes care of my father? I don't mean just cooking and cleaning, which we all do, but you know what I mean— " and she'd lower her voice to a whisper so that men wouldn't hear her in the other room, "—one has to be a whore for her husband! And that's what I cannot bring myself to become!"

My brother believes that Tuba was a whore from the beginning. Grandfather saw her in a bar or even a whorehouse and fell for her. A whore from the beginning or not, there were rumors that Tuba opened a whorehouse when she divorced Grandfather. We were all shocked—first the divorce and then this business they were talking about. Tuba and Grandfather had lived together for thirteen years; they had gotten old together. What had happened?

The divorce was sudden. Grandfather and Tuba disappeared for a month and then Grandfather appeared without his wife. The gossips said that the couple went to a resort together, Tuba fell in love with a young boatman or fisherman or something, dumped Grandfather, and sailed with the young man to the Arabian Islands. Anyway, no one heard of Tuba for a while. Then one of my uncles (the one with a reputation as a gambler and womanizer) brought the news that Tuba had opened a fancy whorehouse in an affluent neighborhood of the city, the neighborhood where all the first-class nightclubs and cabarets were located.

Several of my uncles and cousins went there to check it out for themselves. I'm not sure if what they really hoped was to make love to Tuba, but they definitely wanted to see her in her new position. My brother was a teenager at that time; I remember very well that he pleaded and begged for hours, but Father didn't let him join the group. The uncles and cousins who went reported that they hadn't seen her, but had seen her girls who were all fabulous, expensive, and exclusive. They said that the girls didn't call her Tuba, they called her Madame. "Madame doesn't live here and doesn't see visitors," the girls said.

"So this is where all our money went." Grand-Lady beat her bony chest, cursed, and moaned when she heard the news. "And all of my son's money. The bitch was planning this all her life. To rob our respectable family and open a whorehouse."

"A curse on her fortune-telling!" Aunty Effat said. She resented Tuba because her son Naser had become a full-fledged police informer. There were rumors that he tortured the political prisoners.

"She sucked Father's marrow, the bitch!" Aunty Monir, who was angry and bitter after her divorce, said. "Look at poor Father, he is as aged as a ninety-year-old, while he's not even seventy!"

This was true. After Tuba's disappearance, Grandfather suddenly aged. But sooner than you would think, he married a respectable lady. This was Grandfather's fourth marriage. The women said that Grandfather married Hajie-Khanoom only because of her twins, Gilla and Villa. These girls were eighteen and supernaturally beautiful. One of them—I'm not sure which one—had colored her long, thick hair blonde to distinguish herself from her sister. They were marvels of femininity, Anita Ekberg doubled, Swedish models, American cover girls.

I remember Grandfather's old age as spent basically in a narrow bed, Hajie-Khanoom serving him food or washing his chamber pot, Gilla and Villa roaming around the bed, chirping and giggling, teasing the old man. Grandfather, who had turned into a passive voyeur, watched the girls brushing their long hair, changing their tight blouses, even smearing lotion on their ivory legs. Women swore that they had seen Grandfather's blanket raise up under his belly when he watched the twins.

No one knows what Grandfather's disease was, but after Tuba's disappearance he didn't get up anymore. He stopped functioning altogether. Some say Hajie-Khanoom married Grandfather to inherit his small savings and government pension, and gradually poisoned him.

Grandfather died only a year after he married the mother of the gorgeous twins. One night he threw up and didn't stop vomiting. In the hospital, with different tubes connected to him, moving blood and yellow liquids into and out of his body, he died, looking like a gray sack of bones. I remember his dentureless mouth, the way his jaw and chin rested, and his skin creased like an old hen's.

At his funeral I was the only person who saw Tuba. No one else noticed her because no one else had studied this woman the way I had. I was standing at the door of the hall as a hostess, looking at the women's section. The mullah's sermon was about Grandfather's moral principles, his charities, his love for his family, and his strong faith in religion. Everyone was listening seriously and nodding in approval. Some were wiping their tears with the corner of their handkerchiefs. That's when I noticed that one woman among them all had a black veil hanging over her face. Women didn't cover their faces in those days. I looked at her from head to foot and my glance lingered on her velvet pumps, glittering with many sequins.

I elbowed my brother who was standing by my side, "Tuba is here! I swear this is her!"

Suddenly the black-veiled woman, as if hearing me, stood up and approached the door. When she passed me, I smelled her rose water and camphor scent. My brother and I followed her into the alley, but she disappeared in the curve of a brick wall like a pale shadow in the absence of the sun. It was windy that day. An early spring wind brought dust in the air. We stood for a moment in the cloud of dust, doubting that a woman had just passed.

No one saw or heard of Tuba after Grandfather's death. No one even talked about her. After a year, Grandfather himself was forgotten. Cousin Naser, the former revolutionary who had turned secret agent, shot his wife and children and blew his own brains out at the outbreak of the revolution. No one remembered Grandfather or Tuba even then. A revolution happened in our country and the new government closed the theaters, concert halls, night clubs, cabarets and whorehouses, and opened mosques, police headquarters, modern prisons, and marriage centers for temporary, but legal, sex. In the first year of the revolution many dancers, singers, entertainers, fortune tellers and whores were executed.

My brother imagines that Tuba ended up in the women's unit of the Castle. He imagines her in a black veil covering her from head to toe, her feet swollen from the lashes of cabled whips. He imagines her at the Wall of the Almighty, the guards pushing her into a burlap sack, tying the top tightly so that she can't tear it open when they're shooting her.

I liked Tuba when I was a child, didn't I? She was ageless, lively, colorful and happy, like a jungle bird. She was different and was proud of her difference. So I like to think that Tuba left the country as many other people did. I like to think that she could afford to bribe the officials, or to pay a drug smuggler to get her across the border. Who knows, after all? Maybe Tuba possessed gold coins in her glands and used them to leave the country. I like to imagine her with the same curly red hair flaming around her face, the same silk shawl with the picture of a weird peacock printed on it.

In my imagination Tuba sits in the foggy red light of a bar in Los Angeles or San Francisco, telling the unbelievable story of her life to a group of half-drunk younger men. Her husky voice and her thick accent are so sexy and exotic that more people gather around her chair. I imagine that all these men desire Tuba, not knowing what an awful long life she has lived. In the dim light, through a cloud of smoke, men gaze at Tuba's red lips, listening to her story, mesmerized, bewitched.

THE DANGER OF GALAPAGOS

We live at the end of the city where the carrousels are. There is a ruined wall here or maybe it was only half built from the beginning. Behind the wall is the water; in front, the carrousels.

The carrousels are set up in a vacant lot. They have been in this lot as long as we can remember. But, they say, before the carrousels, people used to dump their garbage here. You can still see a few trash dumpsters around the lot.

You don't find many people riding. A few children come every evening. These children are from the houses that are complete and they all speak the same language. The children of the incomplete houses, who speak different languages, cannot ride on the carrousels. Each ride costs a coin. These children, the ones with different languages, hang around the dumpsters or stare at those who ride the carrousels. Some old trucks always park around the lot. The men of the complete houses, whose children are on the carrousels, drink beer while waiting for them to finish their ride. But most of the time the carrousels are empty.

They are very old. The white of the wooden horses has become a murky gray. The metal airplanes have rusted from wind and rain. The little cars that move up and down have turned into shapeless containers. The mechanical waltz of the white horses is scratchy and there are gaps between the notes.

This is the end of the city. There is a ruined wall here. The wall could have been a brick wall or a cement wall, but now it's impossible to tell what material it was made from. It could have been a good wall, had they completed it. It's either half-completed or ruined. Maybe it was ruined by an earthquake, a flood, or simply age.

Water is behind the wall. It cannot be seen. Not that the wall is high. As low as it is, it still conceals the water. But if one climbs the wall or goes up on top of a roof, or rides on the tallest carrousel, he can see the water. But nobody wants to. The children who ride the carrousels always see the water.

We saw the water once. I think everybody has seen it at least once. Once is enough. The water was dark and greasy and extended to a black horizon. We don't know where that black horizon is. They say the ships spill oil in the water. But nobody has seen a ship or even heard a ship's horn.

But trains pass frequently, and they whistle. They pass along the length of the wall, from east to west or west to east. These are not passenger trains. They don't have windows. They are freight trains. The gondola cars are rusty and you cannot read the name of the company. Nobody knows what they carry to the west or east.

Here at the end of the city the streets are short. They end at the wall. There is the sign "Dead End" at the beginning of each street. The houses are either complete or incomplete. Some of the complete houses have roofs, rooms, kitchens and yards. Incomplete houses lack at least one of these.

Our neighbor's house lacks a roof. When we first moved here, the old man had a roof with a big hole in it. Still, he could stay in his house. He would stay in the right side of the house, which still had a roof. He would avoid the left side. When the left side was wet from rain, the right side was fine. The floor of the left side was covered with buckets and tubs. He collected the rain water and put it in the yard along the wall. We don't know why. We never saw him using the rain water. It was hard for the old man to carry the heavy buckets out and bring empty buckets in. It rains a lot here. So he brought a broken bathtub he found in the dumpster and put it under the broken roof.

With the big storm, the rest of the old man's roof flew away. The morning after the storm we found black shingles and pieces of roof all over the street, in our yard, even inside our house. For months we found shingles everywhere. "What is this black thing in my soup?" one of us would ask. "Oh, it's the old man's shingle." "What are these dark and greasy things sticking to the white sheets?" one of us would wonder. "Oh, they are the old man's shingles." "What is this tarred piece of wood in my pocket?" "It's the old man's shingle."

Now the old man sits in his house under the sky. On sunny days he sips his beer or even invites his drinking friends over. They mainly talk about the lost roof, how it was complete long ago, then lost its completeness, got holes in it, the right side sunny, the left side rainy, and then the storm. They chat and sometimes even laugh. But on rainy days the old man is alone. He holds an umbrella over his head and sits in the middle of the house. When it rains too hard he moves to a nearby factory and sits under the eaves.

Factories are all around. Some are very old, made of red brick. They have small windows, mostly broken. Some are new, with tall cement walls; they are solid and strong. But we have never seen workers going to work or coming back, workers with blue overalls and lunch bags. The factories must be vacant.

But the bars are not vacant. At the corner of each short street, which leads to the wall, there is a bar. They are not busy, but if you peek in you can see a few people inside the red fog. Sometimes we see very old women. They might be the residents of the complete houses whose grandchildren are on the carrousels, turning and looking at the dark water. These old women stand at the open doors of the bars. Some have orange hair, stale powder on their faces, red circles on their wrinkled cheeks. They gaze into a vacant spot in twilight.

    Dogs are loose here, even dogs of the complete houses. They are muddy; they roll in the puddles of rain and tear the garbage bags. If we ever walk in our street—which we normally avoid—the dogs rub their muddy muzzles on our white, starched pants, or our bare, freshly soaped calves. They bark all night long. They mate or fight and tear the cats up.

    People fight too. Mostly at night. Both people of the complete houses and people of the incomplete ones. The neighbor across the street screams every night. She curses someone. Her strong voice goes all the way down to the end of the dead end, hits the wall like a hollow ball and returns. She cries, pleads, begs, curses, breaks breakable objects, then is quiet. But only for a few minutes. Then she starts all over again. Sometimes her cries and curses are like a song, even have a rhythm, or maybe a melody. She lives with a man in one of the complete houses. We have never seen them. They never come out in daytime. They live at night.

Nobody knows anybody's name here. We refer to everybody this way: "the old man whose roof flew away " or "the woman who curses at night." There is a house at the corner of the street opposite the dead end sign. It's the lame man's house. The lame man, his fat wife and seven children live in one of the incomplete houses. Their house is fine but doesn't have a kitchen. When we pass their small side yard (they don't have a front or back yard, they have a side yard), we see an old refrigerator, a gas stove and a kitchen cabinet in the grass. The fat woman cooks outside. On sunny days she looks happy and smiles at the passers-by. On rainy days she holds her umbrella with one hand and stirs the onions with the other. She doesn't even nod. Seven boys and girls come back from school and with their bare feet splash the rain water on each other. The first four are big enough to be called adults. The last one is very small. They all go inside, one by one. We wonder how they fit in a one-room house.

The lame man doesn't work. From morning to evening he limps up and down the street with a crutch under his right armpit, looking up at the sky to see if it's cloudy or not, looking around at the houses. We think he counts the number of the complete and incomplete houses. He may be investigating the missing items: what this house is missing, what that house. What if they could put several houses together and make a complete one, he may wonder. On rainy days he joins the old roofless man under the factory shelter. The old man drinks, but he doesn't. They both stare at the black curtain of the rain.

There are other incomplete houses that have nice large kitchens, but don't have rooms. There are four rented houses across the street, identical, but each a different color. The yellow house, the blue one, the red one, and the cream one. The colors are always fresh and shine on sunny days. Someone (the landlord maybe, a short man with thick black mustachios), comes every month and paints all four houses. The residents open the door and step into the kitchen and that's all. No room to the right or left or at the end of the house. They cook there and sleep there. They pee in a vacant lot behind their house. These houses look like tiny match boxes; they look complete, but they are not. We can't decide who is happier, the lame man and his family, who don't have a kitchen, or the residents of the match boxes who live in kitchens.

We live in the most complete house on the street. It has everything, even a basement. But our house wasn't complete in the beginning. We completed it. It didn't have a fence or gate and it wasn't in the same row with the other houses, it was set farther back. So people walking from the beginning of the street to the wall, or from the wall to the beginning of the street, always turned into our yard, assuming that it was a cul-de-sac. They walked on our grass and saw us hanging out our white sheets, cleaning dead animals out of our basement, or collecting the old man's shingles in a garbage bag. So we bought a tall cedar fence and a nice cedar gate and hid behind them.

But we wish our house didn't have this basement. When it rains, water creeps in from the little mouse holes inside the walls. The basement becomes a stagnant pool. We close the door tight to keep the water in. We don't want it to flow into the yard and break the nice cedar gate. All night long on rainy nights we hear the toads singing in the pool. When it rains for many days, lizards, fish, and other sea animals swim here.

Once it rained nonstop for two weeks. We heard a large turtle gulping the murky water. We got worried: "What if it grows into a Galapagos?" We had read in the encyclopedia that the Galapagos turtle grows in the rain. It can get as large as a house. But the rain stopped before the turtle became a Galapagos. The pool dried up and we had to clean up the dead animals. But it rained again and they started to live under us. We filled the mouse holes several times. Mice dug new ones.

The pool worries us. On rainy nights we think, What if the water comes up, what if we sink down? What if the turtle grows into a Galapagos? What if we wake up in the morning and find our mattresses floating on the water? What if the water breaks the basement door, then the new gate, and flows out of our house, becomes a river, runs toward the end of the street and breaks the half-ruined wall? What if this river, originating from our basement, with us floating on it, joins the big, dark water behind the wall and takes us to the unknown black horizon? What if we take everybody with us? We feel responsible. We are worried. The residents of our neighborhood, both in their complete or incomplete houses, if not happy, are content. They have lived this way for a long time, since before the carrousels. We don't want the little pool in our basement to become a river, ruin the people's houses and take them to the water behind the wall.

All night long, on rainy nights, when the long whistle of the train is muffled by the sound of the rain, we toss and turn on our damp mattresses and murmur, "What if...? What if...?" That's all we think. When we hear the little tides hit the basement's old door and the toads sing and the lizards dive in and out of the mouse holes, especially when the large turtle gulps the water and gets larger and larger, almost the size of a Galapagos, we sit in our beds, erect, pale and shaky, we look through the wet window panes, at the curtain of rain, and whisper, "What if...? What if... ?"

On these nights of worry and insomnia, the noises inside our house, the noises of our contaminated pool, cover the noises from outside: the bark of the muddy dogs, the cry of the cursing woman, and the squeaky sound of the carrousels which, in spite of everything, turn around and around, empty under the heavy rain, their waltzes rusty and old.

THE CRAZY DERVISH AND THE POMEGRANATE TREE: A MYSTIC TALE

"Under nine layers of illusion, whatever the light, on the face of any object, in the ground itself, I see your face."

—Jelaluddin Rumi

In the rose garden outside the monument of one of the two great poets of Raz—not the wise one, but the one who was a great lover—very close to the marble shrine, there is a small grave marked by a cracked gray stone. The epitaph is washed out from wind and rain and cannot help the visitors. The guides explain that this is the crazy dervish's grave. If the visitors ask, "Who was this dervish?" they simply say, "He lived once, in this monument, loved the great lover, and died here." They don't know more.

An old pomegranate tree protects the dervish's miserable grave from the strong sun of Raz. The lower part of the tree looks dried and dead, but the top glows with life. The right side bears no fruit; it's the left side that is always heavy with ripe, red pomegranates. When the fruits are filled with juice, they fall on the gray stone and crack open; thousands of ruby red seeds spread over the grave, like little bleeding hearts. The pomegranate juice runs over the cracked stone like the fresh blood of an ancient sacrifice. A sour, sweet smell—like the smell of love itself—fills the garden of the lover poet and wins over the sweet scent of the roses.

Raz is the city of wine and roses; pomegranates, the fruit of the desert, do not grow here. This tree is the only one of its kind.

More than a thousand kilometers away, in a desert not far from Rey, the capital city, there is a colony of pomegranate trees—a small orchard in the middle of nowhere. These trees, too, are part dead and part alive. Those who have seen this pomegranate colony and the single tree above the sorry grave in the city of Raz cannot doubt that the isolated tree belongs to this colony. The distance of a thousand kilometers puzzles them.

The tale of the dervish, the two poets, and the pomegranate tree might have been like this:

Once there lived a dervish in the city of Raz. This city was as small as a town, but as important as Rey, the capital. It was important because of its wine and oil, poetry and industry. The city was divided in two: the Rose City and the Gas City. The Rose City was where the tombs of the two famous poets were—both lived and died seven hundred fifty years before the dervish. One of the two poets was the poet of wisdom, the other, the poet of love.

Although the love-worshipping people of Raz regarded the lover more highly, they had an immense respect for the wise one, who himself was in love with life and had acquired his wisdom by plunging himself into life's turbulent sea.

In the Rose City, most of the people grew grape vines and made red wine in their cellars. Two thirds of the population were poets, some professional and published, some illiterate but equally talented. The second group's oral poetry was often more popular than the first group's written. The tailor was a poet, the grocer a poet, the shoemaker the same, and the street sweeper, too.

In the other part of the city, the Gas City, was a huge refinery. Workers' rundown huts and hovels stretched along the narrow alleys surrounding the jungle of tangled pipes and forest of tall derricks. In the gas part, the torches burned all day and night, and the smell of oil and gas made the passersby sick. The Gas City produced the wealth of the whole country but was the poorest part of the land. It was much poorer than the Rose City, which produced only wine, rose water, and poetry. The people of Gas didn't have time to think or to sleep the deep sleep that allows a human being to dream. They didn't know what poetry was. The Alley of Shaitan was a narrow, muddy alley in the Gas City where the prostitutes' hovels stretched along a smelly gutter that carried human waste.

Now the dervish lived in the rose part of the city of Raz. Some said he had been a merchant once, had given up his properties and divorced the world—a wine merchant maybe, or a rose water dealer—there were different versions of his previous life. Some even claimed that he had been a prince once and lost his sanity over the love of a woman. When she left him he abandoned his castle and family to search for her. Half naked, he roamed the world but couldn't find her, and returned as a dervish.

He wore a white Caftan like a shroud, and lived in the monument of the lover poet. The monument was circular in shape and a white dome sat on its top. The poet's white marble tomb was under the dome. The dervish slept on top of the tombstone and the strange indigo sky of Raz glared through the columns that enclosed them— him and the lover poet. All day, every day, the poor dervish roamed the streets of Raz along the Roman pines and rose beds and murmured something which some thought was the lost woman's name and some imagined was one of the many names of God.

The dervish was barefoot, his hair and beard, salt and pepper, down to his waist. He didn't have a brass bowl, like many dervishes had, to beg for money, nor had he a bell to announce his presence, nor even a green shawl around his head to protect him from the strong sun of Raz and to show that his ancestor was the last prophet. All the dervish had in the universe was a white shroud to cover his nakedness.

In the crooked streets of Raz, the dervish walked and walked and walked some more. In the tangled maze of the bazaar, he roamed without looking at the glittering objects around him. Then he returned to the monument, to the lover, to rest. At this hour, the historic sight was closed to people. He went inside, under the dome, sat there by the tomb, and reflected on or recited some of the poet's ghazals. Some said he danced alone at times, turned and spun like a top, rotated around the marble tomb, repeating one of the many names of God. Some said he repeated the woman's name.

Only once in a long while did people see the dervish residing in the monument of the wise poet. The wise poet's tombstone was made of black marble and was on top of a square black platform. Black marble columns surrounded the area. The wine-loving, love-seeking people of Raz believed that the dervish needed wisdom only once in a long while.

The dervish dreamed of a pomegranate tree when he was sleeping on the cold white marble one night. The lover was under him, all ashes and bones. This tree he dreamed about was in the gas part of the city, where he had never been. It was growing out of mud and excrement which ran over the ground in front of the prostitutes' and workers' hovels. The tree was both ugly and beautiful. The lower part was rotten, sitting in the sewer, the top was a heavenly sight. Large, red, juicy pomegranates hung from the branches like red lanterns, the ruby-like seeds inside marvels of nature. Each fruit contained hundreds of transparent red gems, sweet and sour as love itself. The dervish saw himself in green silk, hair and beard black and perfumed, stretching his arm up to pick a fruit. But the red lantern of the fruit was on the highest branch and his arm could not reach it.

This is the sign of "It," the Truth, God, the dervish told himself. I'm not searching enough. I have to go to the bazaar and find the entrance to the Gas City. This is where the tree is.

The day after the dream, he went to the bazaar and walked through the maze, but could not find the entrance to the Gas City. He trudged through the narrow alleys, looked into the chambers and small shops on either side with the hope that he would see a sign. In the alley of the perfume sellers, he almost fainted from the strength of the scents. In the alley of the silk merchants, the glitter of Chinese silk almost blinded his eyes. He passed the alleys of Persian carpets, Egyptian jewelry, Arabian spices, African herbs, Afghani dried fruits, and whatnot. The dervish was dizzy and lost. This was the first time he had opened his senses to sights and smells. Before, he would pass the alleys, closed into himself, hidden behind the many folds of his soul like a secret word inside a sacred book.

The first day, the dervish got lost, could not find the entrance to the gas part of the city, and stepped out of the bazaar into the rose part again and returned to his tomb. He dreamed the same dream that night and the next day returned to the bazaar. The second day, he got lost again. The third day, he got even more lost. He couldn't find either of the entrances: the one to the gas part, which he was seeking, and the one to the rose part, where he had entered. In the middle of one of the narrower corridors of the bazaar, which grew like a thin branch out of a thicker one, he lay down on the bare brick floor. The shops were closed. Big locks hung on the wooden double doors. This was the alley of the tanners and the strong unpleasant odor of animal skins kept him awake all night. Many times the dervish felt nauseated and wanted to vomit. He lay on his back, took short breaths, and gazed at the small eye of a window on the tall, arched ceiling, far away from him. Outside, the night was as dark as tar.

The dervish thought that spending the night in the tanners' bazaar was his destiny. It was meant for him to feel sick and stay up all night and see visions. He saw the vision of the pomegranate tree without being asleep—the same tree, rooted deep in rot, but growing glittering red fruits, each containing hundreds of juicy ruby seeds.

All night long, the dervish stretched himself up on his toes like a dancer to grab a fruit, but the fruit was high up and his arms were short. With the first beam of the dawn that linked the sky and the brick floor by a straight phosphorescent column of light, he touched one of the pomegranates, and it was so ripe that it fell and rolled on the floor. The fruit whirled and swirled like a globe of fire and the dervish followed it like a little boy chasing his ball. The fruit rolled out the entrance of the bazaar. All this time the entrance had been just a few steps away from him and he couldn't see it because of the dark. The dervish interpreted this as "Truth" being only a few steps away, within reach but not within reach, he so close to it but not seeing it because of his ignorance.

He stepped out and saw the Gas City.

In the thick blue of the dawn, when the sky is more dark than light, the thousand torches of the refinery glowed like a jungle on fire. The dervish gazed at the orange horizon and followed the pomegranate. He found himself in a mud-covered narrow alley, the Alley of Shaitan. He walked ankle deep in the mess and stepped in the gutter filled with excrement. He looked at the hovels and huts and saw crooked windows, each framing a woman's face. Red and black paint ran down and dripped off the exhausted, sleep-deprived faces. But the last window of the last hovel framed an unpainted face—peaceful and painless, serene. This woman had the beauty of a cloudless sky and the dervish was puzzled by the contrast between the image of a fiery, blood-dripping pomegranate and this other of a vast tranquil blue—the sea, the sky itself.

He stopped and looked up. He couldn't be mistaken. This woman was the promised pomegranate tree. She was "It" in one of its many shapes. The top part was heavenly, and the bottom part...? He had to see the woman's lower half. He couldn't go back without seeing it. He had searched all his life to find "It" and now could not leave without seeing it all.

He fought his doubts. What if this is not "love" but human desire? What if she is not "It" but a woman and he simply wanted to look at her? He returned. But he didn't sleep in the lover's monument; he was angry with the poet for tempting him with an earthly love. He went to the wise poet's grave and slept on the cold, black marble. He dreamed of the pomegranate tree, each fruit burning like a ball of fire. The wise poet told him, "You sought it and found it. Don't let it rot!"

The next day the dervish begged some money in the bazaar and went to the Alley of Shaitan, to the whorehouse.

"This one is just for display," the lady of the house said. "She doesn't have anything from the waist down!" She laughed loudly, shamelessly.

The dervish insisted. The women of the house all gathered around him, pointed their fingers at him, ridiculed him. He paid his few coins and entered.

"Her name is Naroo," the lady yelled, while he was climbing the narrow crooked stone steps.

The dervish's heart sank, for he knew that in the Razian dialect Naroo had a double meaning: fire and pomegranate. He climbed the steps like a young lad and rushed into Naroo's room. Her back was to him, her face to the window. She was strapped to a wooden chair; she could not move. The dervish lifted the chair and turned it toward him. The ragged blanket on Naroo's lower half fell to the floor and he saw that she had only a torso and nothing more. The women had wrapped her bottom in a black rag.

The dervish sat cross-legged, facing the half-woman, her chest strapped to the chair. He sighed and cried and murmured to himself. Naroo blinked and when she breathed, one strand of her long honey-colored hair quivered. These signs proved that she was alive.

The dervish took a brass bowl and went begging. He begged just enough to be able to go to Naroo, sit with her and worship her. The women of the house peeked through the keyhole and muffled their giggles. They called him the Crazy Dervish.

The dervish didn't dream of the pomegranate tree again.

One cold night, when the dervish was lying on the frozen white marble, resurrecting Naroo's face in his mind as he did every night to feel warm and secure, strange noises blurred his vision and interrupted his meditation. He ran out of the monument and saw people running around in panic. A young man who had covered his face with a white scarf said, "Father, hide! This is war; they call it a revolution. Hide, else you'll be killed!"

Instead of hiding, the old lover rushed to the Gas City where his beloved was. Now, after months of visiting Naroo, the dervish knew his way very well. He knew all the crooked alleys of the bazaar like the lines of his own palm. He knew where the entrance to the other city was. He reached the Alley of Shaitan and saw men carrying black flags, pulling the women out of the hovels. The shrieks and cries of the women begging for help broke the dervish's heart. But how could he fight against hundreds of men, all armed with guns of a kind he had never seen before?

The crowd gathered around the women and made a circular stage. The Black-Flaggers dragged the women and dropped them in the mess and the mud. The leader of the group took a stone and hit a woman and others took stones and hit the women. The people—some stoned and some didn't. The dervish looked up. Naroo's window was empty. For a second he hoped that she had stopped breathing. Yes, he wished her death. She would be better off dead, not to have to suffer.

But they threw the chair out of the house with Naroo strapped to it. She and the chair landed sideways on the mud. The left part of her face lay in the gutter, the right side up. As the first man stoned Naroo, the dervish, brisk as a young lad, grabbed a gun and shot him and many others. He didn't know that this gun could shoot so many bullets with a single touch of the finger. At least ten Black-Flaggers fell; the others chained the crazy dervish and took him away.

In his cell, the dervish fasted in order to die. How could he know where Naroo was or if she was alive? He moaned inside his throat and rocked himself in pain. Young prisoners watched him with wonder. "What is this old dervish doing here? Why have they brought an old man?" Someone who had witnessed what the dervish had done told the account of his bravery to the others. The youth respected him, cherished him, and fasted with him. His fasting, which inspired the other inmates, brought some privileges to the prisoners. The Black-Flaggers were forced to give them time to shower, soap, and better soup.

The inmates stopped fasting, but the dervish went on.

One young man, who always covered his face with a white scarf, in the middle of the night crawled toward the dervish and whispered in his ear, "Do you believe that sometimes a young person can advise an old one?"

The dervish nodded.

"You taught me that in love one has to be persistent, but now I want to give you advice. Don't give up; stay alive and fight! Have you given up?"

The dervish shook his head, meaning "No."

"Then break your fast," the young man said, "You don't want to die, do you?"

The dervish shook his head.

"If you stay alive, you may go out and find her."

The old dervish never saw the youth's face, but his warm voice stayed in his ears. He stopped fasting in the hope of release.

The crazy dervish sat silently in his cell for a long time. He witnessed the torture and killing of his twenty-four inmates. The guards killed the veiled youth, too. In the dervish's dark and confused dreams, the picture of Naroo—still clear and fresh as the morning sun—mixed and mingled with the bloody images of these boys. When a cellmate went to the Wall of the Almighty and the dervish heard the rattle of the machine guns, he dreamed of the pomegranate tree that night, legs in the mud and head in the glowing sun, ruby-red fruits glittering like gems. But one fruit would crack open and bleed to death.

The dervish never heard the voices of the poets in his dreams, but occasionally he envisioned their cold and quiet tombstones.

Love and wisdom have both divorced me, he thought.

Years passed. Youth came into the cell and youth

went out to the Wall of the Almighty. The old dervish stayed in the same corner, at times murmuring, at times mute. The Black-Flaggers were tired of him. "Why feed a crazy, worthless dervish who won't spy on the others, doesn't repent and doesn't die, either? He is not even worth a bullet."

One evening, they put him in a black van, drove a long distance, and threw him out in the middle of a dirt road.

It was dusk. The dervish inhaled the spring air. Although the air didn't have the scent of the roses of Raz, it had the smell of the desert, the dry aroma of earth and wind, the familiar smell of his motherland. He walked along the road toward the horizon, where the sun was setting. He decided that Raz was where the sun sets. Soon he gained back the skill of walking. He found a stick and made himself a cane. After a while, a truck stopped for him.

"Where?" the driver asked, his face wrapped because of the dust and his body hidden in the falling shadows of the night.

"Raz," the dervish said.

"Come up, old man!" the driver said.

The crazy dervish was right; this road of the setting sun stretched to the ancient city.

With all the pepper wiped out of his hair, with salt covering the strands, with his beard down to his knees, with his caftan become a rag, he stepped out of the truck at the first alley of the Gas City, the Alley of Shaitan.

"Don't you want to go to the Rose City?" the driver asked.

"No. Here is my home," the dervish answered.

Along the length of the Alley of Shaitan, now called the Alley of the Holy One, the beaten hovels were still sitting in the mud. They were clumsily painted white. Black curtains covered the windows. A Black-Flagger sat on a stool at the entrance of the first hovel, fingering his nose.

"What do you want, Father?" he asked.

"Where is this place?" the dervish asked.

The soldier laughed and showed his slimy teeth. "This is the Marriage House, Father. Too late for you." He laughed some more.

"Marriage House?" The dervish had never heard of such a thing before.

"You get a ticket, you go in, pick a woman, marry her for an hour or two, do what you need to do, and leave. Temporary marriage, that's what it is. Interested?" The soldier showed his yellow teeth again.

"Do you have Naroo here?" the dervish asked.

"Naroo? Naroo who? What does she look

like?" the soldier asked.

The dervish couldn't describe her. How could he define "It" in words?

"Listen," the soldier said, "If your daughter is here, it's going to cost you money to get her out." He rubbed his fingers together. "How much can you spend? I'll get her out if you pay me a tip. But you're all in rags." And he turned his back.

"Naroo was her name and she was strapped to a chair," the dervish mumbled.

"Her? Oh, she is married now. Permanently. Too late," the soldier said.

"Married?"

"Married to the Big Sheikh, head of all the muezzins. His house is in the Rose City, behind the mosque."

The old dervish took the short cut through the bazaar. After so many years, he walked on the brick floor of the tangled alleys again. He inhaled the aroma of saffron and cinnamon, turmeric, and dried lemon. He opened his senses to all the sights and smells. He touched the garments as he passed the alley of the silk merchants. He looked in all the mirrors in the alley of the mirror makers. He wanted to come back to life, sharpen his senses in his old age, to be able to see her—Naroo.

When he stepped out of the bazaar a sudden shock stopped him. He couldn't go farther. All of the tall Roman pines on either side of Rose Boulevard were dry from head to foot. They were yellow, a marvel for the sight. The rose bushes were gone and, instead, small black flags were planted in their former flower beds. The people of Raz bent their heads, looked at the tips of their shoes, walking as though searching for something lost. The women, the lively, loving, love-seeking women of Raz, were shrouded in black; they looked like enormous, wingless bats.

The dervish went to the tomb of the poet, the lover. There was a tall barbed-wire fence around the monument with a thick iron gate. The white dome and the white marble tombstone were hidden inside. Two Black-Flaggers guarded the gate.

The dervish approached and said, "Let me in."

They prodded him with the butt of their guns.

"Let me in. This is where I live."

They beat him up and threw him in the gutter.

Bloody and beaten, the dervish trudged to the wise poet's monument. He saw the same fence, gate, and guards. He stood in the shade of a yellow pine and sighed. "Love and wisdom, both locked in, how am I ever to find Naroo?" He sat there, laid his tired head on the dried trunk of a dead pine and cried soundlessly until he fell asleep.

Naroo came to him in his dream. She was on her chair, straps across her chest, her old blanket covering her from the waist down, one strand of her honey-colored hair quivering faintly when she exhaled.

"She is alive! She is alive!" the dervish screamed in his dream. Now she was there and then she wasn't. Instead, there was the pomegranate tree, feet in mud and excrement and head near the sun. The heavy branches motioned to him to come.

The dervish woke up and in the fresh spring evening of Raz (the breeze was still fragrant with the memory of rose and wine), he walked toward the mosque and, without searching, found the house of the Big Sheikh. It was the biggest and the whitest of all the houses. He roamed around and hid behind the turquoise minaret to watch. A carriage approached, the Big Sheikh sitting in the car, Naroo at his side, her soft, shining hair covering half her face. The crazy dervish blinked and rubbed his eyes. This must be a vision, for women cannot show their hair anymore. Vision or not, there she was, part of her face concealed by her silky hair. With the eye uncurtained by her hair, she indicated to him to follow. He received the signal and gained his strength back.

That night, the old dervish divided his time between the lover and the wise. Half the night he lay behind the fence of the lover's monument and half resided outside the wise poet's tomb. Naked, on naked earth, he lay and turned his back to the city and faced the fence. Through the lines of barbed-wire, he saw the glow of the white or the glitter of the black marble stones. He moaned and cried and called the poets' names. He scratched and clawed the moist dirt. He mourned the imprisonment of love and wisdom. He didn't sleep at all. In the morning he borrowed a bowl from another beggar and set out to beg.

Raz was full of beggars now—all looked like the dervish. Young or old, they wore rags and carried brass bowls in their hands. Some were former wine merchants, some poets or perfume sellers, some gone crazy from not being able to see women's faces. The dervish sat in front of the mosque with his brass bowl; he became one in the long row of beggars.

In the evening the bowl was full. The dervish went to the bazaar and bought himself a robe and a pair of sandals. He went to the public bath and washed himself, trimmed his hair and beard and put the new clothes on.

The dervish went to the Sheikh's public dinner—the charity dinner on the Sacred Friday.

He ate and listened to the prayers coming out of full stomachs, mixed and mingled with belch and burp. He lay down in the yard with the other guests and in the middle of the night, when the men's swollen bellies moved gently up and down and each and every one snored or whistled in deep sleep, dreaming of food or of emptying their bowels, he stepped into the Sheikh's house where the women were kept. If they caught him, they would behead him on the spot. But, as though invisible, he entered the harem. The Big Sheikh's wives were all asleep, except Naroo who was strapped into a golden chair, looking out at a tall yellow pine piercing the inky sky. The dervish unfastened Naroo from the chair and hid her under his wide robe. A short while later, they were on the dirt road heading toward the horizon, where the sun would rise.

Naroo breathed under the dervish's robe and her heart beat on the dervish's heart and the old man, gaining strength from Naroo's pounding heart, became young again and danced in the desert with joy. As there was no tree, no column, no pole, nothing vertical to rotate around, the crazy dervish turned around himself and chanted, "Naroo! Naroo!" And Naroo laughed and cried under the dervish's robe, or he thought that she laughed and cried.

The dervish traveled all the way to the east, where the sun rose. He sold his sandals and bought bread. They slept in the courtyards of the caravansaries and no one knew there were two hearts beating inside the old dervish's robe. At the end of the land where a line marked the border of the country, the dervish stopped at the clay hut of a shepherd.

The shepherd called him in and offered him hot steaming tea and home-baked bread. He said, "Take the pomegranate out of your robe, dervish, it's not good to keep a fresh fruit wrapped all the time, it will rot."

The dervish took Naroo out.

The shepherd's wife washed her and combed her long honey-colored hair and wrapped her lower part in a clean rag. Now she lay her on a pillow like an imaginary baby or a china doll. The dervish trusted the shepherd and his wife. The shepherd had a warm voice which was familiar to the dervish's ears, especially when he lowered it to a whisper. It was as though the dervish had been with this man somewhere, or even lived with him a long time, in another life.

The dervish told the shepherd that he was seeking a place to live with Naroo—for now and maybe forever. The shepherd pointed his forefinger toward the other side of the ditch. He told him that he could build a little hut and take his bride there. That spot was neither here nor there, didn't belong anywhere. It was no man's land.

With the help of the shepherd and his wife, the dervish built a little clay hut in no man's land and lived there with Naroo, now free of straps all day and night. She lay on a pillow gazing at the endless desert, which moved like an ocean all day, and slept peacefully under the dervish's robe all night. Their hearts lay on one another, pulses gradually merging into one.

The dervish and Naroo lived as the shepherd's neighbors for years. The old man wished for a longer life and his wish was granted. He never dreamed of the pomegranate tree, but every night he dreamed of the two tombstones—the white marble and the black marble—in the remote city of Raz. He missed his city and the two poets so much, he cried in his dreams. Naroo woke up on his chest and lay her cool hand on his burning forehead until he became quiet.

The Black-Flaggers spied on the dervish's hut with binoculars and even tried to shoot him. They never found out he was living with half a woman. They thought he had sought refuge in no man's land because of his opposition to the Holy Government. They took his file from the prison's records and studied it, but after a while they left him alone. He was a crazy dervish, not worth a bullet, they thought.

But a war broke out between the Holy Government and the eastern neighbor. Flashes of light, balls of fire, meteors of rockets, sparks and flames flew all night over the heads of Naroo and the dervish. They hid in their hut and covered their ears. The sounds were deafening. The shepherd told the dervish that his place was not safe anymore and if they stayed they would be killed. But the old dervish had nowhere to go. In his homeland they would take Naroo away from him, in the enemy's land they would kill them both. He stayed, but lost his beloved. One night, an iron-winged bird pierced Naroo's heart. She died on the dervish's chest.

The next morning, the dervish put Naroo in a sack and hung the sack on his shoulder, cut off his beard and the hair which he had never before cut, and changed from his robe into common clothes the shepherd provided him. He passed the battle's front and set forth on the road to the west.

On his way to Raz, the dervish passed Rey, the capital. On the outskirts of the dark smoking city, there was a big hole, the size of a dried pool, with many black-veiled women sitting around it, rocking themselves back and forth, clutching their hair, clawing at their faces and moaning. He inquired; they said this was where the Black-Flaggers threw the corpses of the youth who were executed in the central prison.

"They don't bury them," they said. "They just throw them in this hole and we are here every day to pour dirt on them."

The dervish sat there among the mothers and mourned with them. Now he mourned for Naroo for the first time since her death. A truck arrived, backed up and tilted its huge container. Hundreds of corpses rolled out and piled into the hole. The women took their shovels and threw dust on the dead, while chanting heart-breaking mourning songs.

Now the dervish remembered his prison time and his twenty-four cellmates and many more who were shot at the Wall of the Almighty. He remembered the young man who whispered into his ear one night and advised him to resist. Had he not listened to him, he would never have lived all these years with his beloved Naroo. So he opened the burlap sack, took Naroo out and laid her in the hole with the other corpses. The mothers buried her along with their sons.

The crazy dervish went to Raz, empty-handed, with empty heart. He ripped his clothes off and roamed the town, naked. He passed the monument of the wise poet, still guarded, and didn't remember him. Wisdom had divorced the dervish.

He reached the monument of the lover poet and sat under the yellow pine. The first and second days, the guards prodded and beat him and chased him away, but he returned and sat in the same spot. The third day, they left him alone. So he remained there, naked, except for a rag the soldiers wrapped around his groin. All day long, he murmured something no one understood and all night long he danced around the yellow pine, chanting something that sounded like "Oo... oo... oo... oo...."

People called him the Crazy Dervish and threw pieces of bread to him.

In his last years, the dervish didn't dream, didn't see visions, didn't remember his past life, didn't mention the name of Naroo. All that remained of his long life were the two last letters of his idol's name: "oo," half of her, meaning "It" in Razian language. He chanted "Oo... oo... oo..." in the dark, while dancing around a dead tree, not knowing why.

When he died, the dervish's corpse remained there for a few days and began to decay. The guards, out of laziness, found an easy way to get rid of the corpse—they dragged him inside the monument and buried him among the dead rose bushes, not far from the poet's marble tombstone.

Years went by and there came a day when the Holy Government, bankrupt in many ways, realized that the monuments of the poets could become a good source of income. They ordered the gates and the barbed wire to be removed and allowed visitors to buy tickets to visit the tombs of both ancient poets. But the monument of the wise poet was ruined beyond repair; they demolished it and built another mosque on the lot. They repaired the monument of the lover poet, pulled the weeds out, planted black flags around the white marble tombstone, set up a box office and opened it to the public.

This is when the faithful Razians put a tombstone over the dervish's grave and carved an inscription on it: "Here lies the Crazy Dervish, who searched for love, never found it, and lost his mind." The people of Raz never knew that in his long life the dervish found love more than once and lost it each time, for reasons beyond his control.

To the amazement of the Razians, who had never in their lives seen a pomegranate tree except in school books, such a tree grew over the crazy dervish's grave. It bore ruby red fruits every year, but the lower part of the tree was rotten and half of the living top bore fruit and half was barren.

Those who traveled to Rey reported that exactly the same kind of tree grew at the outskirts of the capital city, but there were many of them there, a colony, an orchard. It was as though the dervish's pomegranate tree in Raz was their sole sister.